The Folly Under the Lake

Salema Nazzal

PNEUMA SPRINGS PUBLISHING UK

First Published in 2015 by:
Pneuma Springs Publishing

The Folly Under the Lake
Copyright © 2015   Salema Nazzal
ISBN13: 9781782284031

Salema Nazzal has asserted her right under the Copyright, Designs and
Patents Act, 1988, to be identified as Author of this Work

British Library Cataloguing in Publication Data. A catalogue record for
this book is available from the British Library.

Cover design by Richard Johnston of www.rjfilmdesign.com

Pneuma Springs Publishing
A Subsidiary of Pneuma Springs Ltd.
7 Groveherst Road, Dartford Kent, DA1 5JD.
E: admin@pneumasprings.co.uk
W: www.pneumasprings.co.uk

for my wonderful children Ziad and Talia

Chapter 1

"We can't possibly turn down an invitation to stay the weekend at Witton Park!" exclaimed Florence Brewer heatedly to her husband Joseph. "Walter and Blanche would be most upset. Walter has spent a small fortune getting the folly built, and he's dying to show it off to us."

"It's not so much a folly as an underwater smoking room by all accounts," mused Joseph, leaning back in his chair, and looking up at the ceiling. "They say the domed roof is made of glass and you can observe the fish swimming by while you're puffing on your pipe. I must say I'm rather keen to view the thing, but a weekend with the Sinnet family is almost more than I can stand. I know he's my father's oldest friend, but the way he constantly clears his throat in that way. He never used to do it and I find it bally annoying. Blanche is pleasant enough but I just can't fathom either of them. I must say, I think…"

"I don't care what you think. We're going and that's final," interrupted Florence, peering at her reflection in her powder compact through half narrowed eyes. "It's not like we're inundated with invitations, though I can't work out why. The word about town is that he's imported some marvellous marble statues that are dotted about all over the estate. I'd like to feast my eyes on them, plus all the improvements he's been making to the house and grounds."

"It certainly sounds like he's been splashing his cash around," said Joseph in a jovial voice. "I've heard the three lakes are quite fascinating."

"Yes I can't wait to see them," said Florence wheeling round with an excited gleam in her eyes. "Apparently the first one is on top of one of Walter's man-made hills. Fancy having so much money that you can move hills around! Anyway, there's a square lake on top of the hill and he's had pipes specially made to cascade water thirty feet down to the next lake."

"That's the bathers' lake I believe," interposed Joseph, squinting through his monocle and then rubbing at the glass with his sleeve.

"That's right. Don't interrupt me Joseph." Florence stood up and moved to the window, gazing out with unseeing eyes, her mind already at Witton Park. "From the bathers' lake there's an eighty-tonne marble dolphin head statue. Imagine that Jo? Eighty tonnes! The water pours through the statue's mouth into the largest lake. That's the one with the folly underneath it. I can't even begin to imagine what it all looks like."

"More money than sense some might say."

"Oh don't be so boring Joseph," snapped Florence. "Anyway, you said you wanted to talk to Walter about investing in Sinnet Industries so we have to go. He told you the investment would be a foolproof venture, and I need to be kept in the style I wish I'd become accustomed to. You seem to be extremely tight with the budget these days."

Joseph raised his eyes to the ceiling and his monocle promptly dropped out. "Well really Florence, what a vulgar thing to say. You knew I had nothing when I married you." He examined his fingernails in a critical manner.

"Yes, well that was five years ago and I've had plenty of time to reconsider," sniffed Florence snapping her powder compact shut and getting to her feet. "Just look at this room. You don't work but you don't even help me keep this place clean."

"My idea of housework is to sweep the room with a glance," chortled Joseph.

"I'm fed up with being poor," continued Florence, ignoring him. "We can jolly well go to Witton Park this weekend, and you can put what little you own into Walter's company, even if it means selling my jewellery. If what he says is true, we'll be rich this time next year." She flounced out of the room leaving a trail of cheap scent in her wake.

"So who's coming this weekend?" Rose asked her brother Harry with interest. "I know Mother has asked Aubrey Sapping up here. I haven't seen him in simply ages. Mother always seems to be recalling antics with her naughty little childhood friend. She should have married him in my opinion, as they are a perfectly suited couple. Must've been fun to have a neighbour of one's age, I've always felt cut off from the world living here. It must be at least seven miles to the village as the crow flies. No one to simply pop by."

"Well I like being cut off," answered Harry with a grin. "No one to bother one."

"That's because you live to read!" interjected his sister huffily. "You may as well ask Father if you can move your bed into the library."

"Not a bad idea," mused Harry looking off into the distance. "It is the perfect hideaway for a bibliophile like me!" He deliberately ignored Rose's dig. "Anyway, you asked who was coming to join our pretty little house party." Harry swept his hand through his thick brown hair and began to count up on his fingers. "Well, we have Jo and Flo for starters."

"Jo and Flo?"

"You know, Joseph and Florence Brewer."

"Oh them!" said Rose, laughing up at her brother and pushing her dark hair out of her face. The curls jumped and sprang back across her cheeks as she moved her head. "Joseph's quite nice but Florence only cares about money and she's so bossy. Can't understand what he sees in her."

"Oh she's alright. They both are in small doses." Harry stood up from where they were sitting by the edge of the lake and looked across its smooth surface towards the house in the distance. "So there are the Brewers and we have cousin Cordelia here already. It's nice to have her here all the way from America, albeit under horrible circumstances. Fancy being made a widow before you're thirty!"

"Simply dreadful, poor thing," said Rose, also standing up and looking in the same direction as her brother. "Shame we never met the chap, he sounded perfect for Cords. I tried talking to her about him last night but she just got up and walked away."

"Still grieving." Harry absent-mindedly skimmed a pebble across the surface of the lake towards the boathouse. "So anyway, who else is there?" He pulled his mind back and shook his head, as if to clear away his current train of thought. "Some Hattie somebody or other. Hattie Atherton or Abberton? Mother vaguely knows her as she's helped her at the women's group in the village and is apparently perfectly charming. She said she's got a kind heart so thought she could be a friend to Cordelia at this time."

"Huh! What about us?" said Rose with a small frown on her pretty elfin-like face. "We are perfect friends for her; if only she'd talk to us."

"I expect she will when she's ready," replied Harry. "I believe I heard Mother say something about a George Brown coming too. He was a possible investor when Father was working out in America and he wants to talk business."

"How simply dull," yawned Rose in a lazy voice. "Business indeed! I was hoping for a bit of fun this weekend, businessmen are invariably bad at letting their hair down."

"Why do you reckon I don't want to join the family business? Father keeps threatening to disinherit me if I don't get involved but I can't stand the thought of it. None of it is quite on the level. He may well have made a fortune promoting those mining companies in America, but it seems that none of the companies have made any money for the shareholders. They are after his blood! Don't quote me but I would imagine that's why Father left America in such a hurry. Anyway, I wouldn't want to be accused of nepotism! Come on, let's get back to the house, it may be sunny, but it looks as if a storm is brewing. Mother will be fussing about the flowers or something equally unimportant. You can go and help her while I go and hide out in the library."

Rose good-naturedly made a face at her older brother and then linked arms with him and they wandered up past the overgrown rhododendrons and back onto the path that led to the house.

Chapter 2

"Aubrey, darling!" Blanche Sinnet welcomed her friend with a smile. "It has been too long. I'm so glad you could make it."

She put down her embroidery and crossed the drawing room to him, unwittingly running her finger across the top of the piano as she passed, and wiping the imaginary dust off on her skirt.

The drawing room was large and airy and steeped in sunshine. Comfortable chairs were dotted about and a large solid table stood in the corner where card games were often played. One window looked out across the neat front lawns and the other one gave the perfect view of the lake.

"As if I wouldn't come," laughed Aubrey, taking her in his arms and waltzing her across the room. "You call and I come running!"

"Oh you daft man. As dippy as ever I see!" Blanche smiled, took her friend by the arm, and led him firmly to the window. "Come and feast your eyes on the lake, it wasn't here last time you stayed. What do you think?"

Aubrey gazed out of the window and took in the scenery before him. "Well I never! Local gossip said that Walter had employed practically the entire village to put a man-made lake here but I could hardly believe it. It's certainly beautiful my dear. I can't even see the sides; it's huge, quite overwhelming! How have those trees and bushes grown up so fast?"

"They were planted that size, you old silly!"

"My goodness that must have cost a small fortune." Aubrey looked a little disapproving. "Is it true about the folly underneath it?"

"Yes," laughed Blanche squeezing his arm. "Walter is very flamboyant with his designs, and once he gets an idea into his head he won't let it go until it's finished. After dinner you can go and look at it, by then it will be all lit up with lights. You see that cherub statue rising up out of the lake over there in the distance? That's the top of the folly roof and it's perched right on top!"

"Well, he is an accomplished chap I must say. The things he comes up with! So much for him being an oil speculator, he seems to have his fingers in every pie you could possibly imagine. Aren't there meant to be some other lakes too?"

"Yes and they're spectacular but you can't see them from the house. If the weather brightens up tomorrow I'll walk you up to them, although I'm not too hopeful. The forecast is dreadful."

"He's very ambitious, your husband, isn't he? What else is he up to at the moment apart from all these huge feats of engineering on your property?"

"I don't know to be honest with you. I can't keep up with him, I'm afraid, and I'm meant to be his wife." Blanche's voice took on a different tone for a second. "I overheard him talking to someone on the telephone the other day about promoting his mining companies on the London market, but who knows? He doesn't seem to tell me a thing these days. I have to hear things through the grapevine to know what he's up to."

"That's not good, my dear. He needs to pay more attention to you."

"Me? I'm the least of his concerns. It's all about business with Walter! He's only just arrived home, having worked in America for ages, but already he's off, and running with some new scheme or other."

"What's the story with that huge wall all around the property with the intimidating spikes on top? I wasn't expecting to see anything like that when I arrived. Is he worried about intruders by any chance?"

"Oh that. Well, Walter seemed to think that as the estate is so big, it would take a lot of time and money to wall it all in. To keep would-be burglars out, he thought he'd safeguard our immediate area. Even an accomplished rock climber would have trouble scaling the height of the walls and gates at the top of the driveway!"

"Yes, those wrought iron gates are something else. You'd need mountaineering equipment for sure! Extraordinary. It all seems a little paranoid, though, if you ask me."

"You may be right." Blanche gazed at Aubrey with unseeing eyes, her thoughts elsewhere for a second. "However, sometimes it feels more than a little claustrophobic."

"Oh darling that's not good. Those driveway gates are beautiful though and I've never seen any that big or ornate before."

"Yes. He designed them himself and had them made by local craftsmen. I guess it was meant to appease the villagers for taking back the fields that they rented from him. He dug up acres of them to make the lake. All this has happened within the last year. Even from America he was arranging changes on the property here, workmen kept appearing, and I had to pretend I was aware of what was happening."

"Apart from all of that, how are you doing, darling? You seem in perfect health, all rosy cheeked and youthful!"

"My goodness, the things you say," said Blanche. "You're good for my health! I'm fine, keeping busy as usual and doing lots of embroidery to sell for the women's work in the village at the moment. It's good to be able to help those less fortunate. What's new with you, Aubrey?"

"Absolutely nothing new. You know how I loathe change! I spend an awful lot of time at my club in town and use my time drinking and lamenting about not being married to you." He had a cheeky glint in his eye.

"What you need is a job; something to keep you out of mischief."

"A job? What a dreadful suggestion, you know there's no need for that kind of talk! Anyway, how are those wonderful children of yours?"

"They are in high spirits as per usual and looking forward to seeing you." Blanche turned away from the window and walked across the room to the door. "Anyway, you're the first to arrive. Let me call Gladys to take you up to your room so you can settle in before dinner. We've put you in your usual room."

"Wouldn't it be simply marvellous to live in a house like this?" chattered Florence in an excited voice. "The conservatory that Walter has added is simply wonderful; quite a design feat I would say. I doubt there's another one like it in all of England. And all those beautiful hothouse plants! It makes one feel as if one were in the tropics, not that I've ever been in the tropics." She looked at Joseph in a reproachful way. She was enjoying the sumptuousness of the bedroom and sniffed at the bowl of flowers on the dressing table in satisfaction. "I shall enjoy being here and dining at someone else's expense this weekend. Did you notice the exquisitely manicured front lawns?"

"I expect they have exquisitely pedicured back lawns too!" brayed Joseph as he tied up his shoes. "My sweet, it's nothing more than bricks and mortar. Who really needs such a lavish house with thirty bedrooms and umpteen bathrooms in it? Living one's life in peace and happiness is surely a far more important pursuit."

"Happiness! It doesn't pay the bills." Florence narrowed her eyes as she looked at her husband and then crossed the room to check on her reflection in the mirror. Her orange blouse, half buttoned, seemed to have had an argument with her patterned skirt.

"You do look nice," said Joseph dutifully, not looking at her.

Florence slipped on her high heels and went to look out of the window. They had a perfect view of the lake. Serene ducks floated across the top, feet paddling furiously below the surface. "How big do you suppose this lake is? I've never seen anything so vast and you can't even see the edges, let alone the other two lakes with their torrents of water crashing into it. Makes one feel rather small."

"I haven't got a clue, but apparently it takes all day to walk around, and there are hidden nooks and crannies to it, with statues and little islands to picnic on."

"How marvellous. I do hope we can row over to one of the islands and take in the views from there. It's a shame Blanche hasn't arranged one of her fetes in the garden for this weekend, as I've heard they're rather fun."

"Fun? Sounds like a 'fete' worse than death to me," snorted Joseph giggling at his own joke. "Anyway, the weather is on the turn so I have an uneasy feeling we may be stuck indoors the whole time."

"Oh, that must be Cordelia down there talking to that rather handsome man. She certainly looks like Blanche, albeit a younger and more beautiful version. What a wonderful fur she has around her shoulders, she must be in the money to afford something like that. Come on, let's go down, and meet the other guests."

Downstairs, everyone was gathering in the plush drawing room to have a pre-dinner drink.

"Welcome one and all! Blanche and I are glad you managed to get here despite the storm warnings. There's one brewing, although it's in actual fact been remarkably calm today."

Walter Sinnet squinted out of the window from his place by the sideboard. He was standing by the silver drinks tray that his discreet butler had brought in and put down. His body was short but broad shouldered with a balding pate and shrewd piercing eyes.

"I hope you get a chance to wander about and see what I've been doing on the estate. Please do go wherever you want to and do let me know what you think of the statues."

"Well I for one love the improvements so far," Florence simpered, almost bobbing down in a little courtesy.

Walter gave her a quick smile that didn't quite meet his eyes. "It has taken many months of meticulous planning and money. I have to say I am very pleased with the outcome so far. There will be more going on so you'll all have to come back again to see what I get up to next!"

Blanche looked at him fleetingly, feeling like a spare part in her own life and then caught Aubrey looking at her from across the room and put on a somewhat forced smile.

"Anyway, what can I get you all to drink?" said Walter looking around at them all. "Cordelia?"

"I'd love a Gibson please Walter." Cordelia drifted over to the sideboard and waited while Walter splashed gin and vermouth into a crystal cut glass and placed a pickled onion inside. He cleared his throat in a noisy way, much to Joseph's chagrin, and handed it to her.

"Cordelia let me introduce you to George Brown. I had a lot of contact with him when I was working in America but this is the first time we've met face to face. We are hoping to do a lot of productive business together, aren't we Mr Brown?"

George had wandered up to them, tall and smartly dressed, with dark blonde hair and glasses. He looked as if he was in his early forties and wore an anxious expression on his face. He put his hand out to shake Cordelia's and she looked up at him and murmured, "How do you do?"

Florence looked at them under her eyelashes. Wasn't this the man she had seen Cordelia talking to in the garden earlier? Why were they pretending to be meeting for the first time now? Before she had the chance to say anything, Blanche, who had gone out when she heard voices in the hall, appeared at the door with a pretty young woman with a sweet face and kind manner about her. She gently propelled her into the centre of the room.

"Everyone, this is Hattie Abberton. I met her at the women's group in the village. She doesn't know anyone here so please be kind!"

Laughing in a self-conscious manner Hattie coloured slightly and smiled around at everyone, her wavy blonde hair fanning out from under her hat. Aubrey, who had been sitting down, got to his feet and stood by Blanche's side in a proprietorial way, handing her a pink gin. He gave Hattie a small smile and asked her how she was.

"Oh I'm very well indeed, thank you."

Harry sauntered over to Hattie, took her hand in his, and smiled. "Hello there." He kissed her hand. "So you're Hattie. Jolly pleased to meet you."

Hattie looked up into kind eyes and smiled back. A little black cat picked his way across the room and sat down at Hattie's feet, waiting to be stroked. She laughed and bent down. "Who is this little fellow then?"

"May I present Pericles, my lady," smiled Harry with a mock bow.

"Ah, Pericles the Greek. Wasn't he responsible for helping democracy to flourish in ancient times?"

"Why yes he was," said Harry in astonishment. "Does history interest you then?"

"It does indeed," replied Hattie smiling. "Particularly Greek. My father got me interested when I was a girl, and I love reading the mythological tales."

"Then you and I are going to get on like a house on fire. History is my biggest passion, along with reading anything and everything I can get my hands on. I have an idea for a historical tome I'd like to write one day, but whether I get round to it or not I have no idea."

"Oh I do hope you do," said Hattie with relish. "I'd read it at once! What will it be about exactly?"

"Myths and fables, and how they translate over to our lives now in the modern world."

"How simply fascinating," said Hattie in a sincere voice.

A short while later the gong sounded and the house party began to drift into the dining room to eat.

Dinner was delicious and Florence, who was unused to so many courses, ate with gusto whilst talking nineteen to the dozen. Despite this, though, she tuned in to as many conversations as she could. There was nothing tastier than a juicy piece of gossip and Florence was never one to go hungry in that area.

Joseph talked to Walter about his father. Blanche and Aubrey sat side by side giggling every now and then. Rose, determined to find something amusing in the businessman, quizzed George about life in America and Harry chatted away to Hattie about books they had both read. He was surprised but relieved to find she loved most of the same ones as him. Only Cordelia sat taking everything in and not saying much. She picked at her roast turkey and occasionally glanced around at her fellow diners with a pale expressionless face.

"But I wanted your father to come this weekend too," Florence overheard Walter saying to Joseph. "It's a shame he's away at the moment, haven't seen the old boy in an age. Is he on business or pleasure?"

"Business, sir," replied Joseph, putting his monocle in. "It always seems to be business these days and I feel he must be worrying about money or something. If only he would slow down and enjoy time with Mother. She must get terribly bored and lonely being on her own so much."

"Bored and lonely?" interrupted Florence dabbing at her mouth with her napkin and picking imaginary cat hairs off her blouse. "How could she be? She has lots of friends. Frankly, there's nothing I'd like better than whiling away the day in my own pursuits while you make money. Your mother should be the happiest woman alive!"

Walter cleared his throat and winced slightly at Florence's words. He turned abruptly away and began a conversation with Aubrey about how successful Sinnet Industries had become.

"Darling..." began Joseph in an undertone, but Florence shushed him and continued shovelling in mouthfuls of food.

Halfway through the meal the butler came up to Walter and coughed in a discreet manner. Walter looked up in annoyance. "Yes, what is it?"

"The storm is picking up, sir. I'm afraid Mr Marlin has decided not to come because of it."

"Right. I see. Well, can you rearrange a day for him to come next week? It's imperative I see him as soon as possible."

"Yes sir." The butler disappeared out of the door.

"Why was Mr Marlin coming, Father?" asked Harry, briefly turning his attention away from Hattie. "I didn't know he was invited this weekend."

"I asked him only yesterday regarding a change I want to make to my will, if you must know," said Walter looking hard at his son and carving his food up viciously with his knife and fork.

"Are you finally cutting me out of it then?" Harry joked in as casual a voice as he could muster up. "You keep threatening to do it."

"What I do with my money is really nothing to do with you." Walter's face had an expression on it that was hard to decipher and Hattie, glancing over, felt a bit nervous of him, and noticed for the first time what thin, cruel looking lips he had.

"I made my money. Every single coin of it was made because of my business acumen. None of it was passed down from my father.

What I wanted I went out and got, and now I shall decide what to do with it when I am no longer around to enjoy it. No one has the right to expect everything handed to them on a plate without working for it."

"Oh. Righto then!" Harry deliberately kept his voice light-hearted and he turned back to face Hattie, who noticed that although he was as attentive as before, his knuckles were white where he was gripping his cutlery too tightly.

Aubrey looked across the table at Walter and began to resume their talk about the business. "I hear you've formed another company, Walter. Haven't you got enough to deal with already?"

Walter looked across at him with a thin-lipped smile. "I have enough to deal with, but making money is in my blood and if I see a gap in the market I fill it. My new company is floating a variety of stock and bonds on the stock exchange."

"I thought I heard that you had had a spot of trouble doing just that overseas."

Walter frowned. "Now wherever did you hear that, I wonder?"

"Just something that came my way by way of the business grapevine," said Aubrey, with a forced smile. "It came to my attention that you may have had to leave America over a scandal of some sort. Now what was it? Wasn't it investors not receiving what was due to them?"

"That is none of your business, Aubrey. I suppose I shouldn't be surprised at your belief in idle gossip about me. You should try listening to the truth as you while away your time in that club of yours."

"Just taking an interest, old chap. I heard that there had been threats made against you and was just enquiring to make sure all was well." Aubrey turned back to Blanche who had gone quiet and was looking down at her plate.

Walter glared at his wife.

Chapter 3

Rose was glad when dinner ended. She had been sitting between her father and George. Her father seemed to speak to her in bullying tones at the best of times and was usually studiously avoided. He seemed to enjoy treating her and her brother in the same way that a cat would play with a mouse. She could tell that he was seething beneath the surface after Aubrey had spoken to him and wished she could have sat somewhere else. George, although polite, was extremely hard to get anything out of. He seemed guarded and kept steering the conversation away from talking about himself. She felt he had something to hide.

"Did you come all the way to England just to do business with my father?"

"Yes." George gave her short shrift. A silence hung between them for a few seconds while Rose waited for him to continue but he clammed up.

"It's a long way to travel," persisted Rose. "For me, in the same situation, I'd have to be absolutely certain before embarking on such a trip."

George looked at her but said nothing.

"So what is it you actually do?" Rose began to get a headache and rubbed her temples with her fingers. Trying to get George to talk was exhausting and she was getting bored of the anxious looking businessman. Besides, he didn't seem to want to ask anything about her at all.

"I deal in jewels," was his short answer and Rose was given no more information. She floundered in her conversation for a while, and then held her hand out towards him, refusing to be beaten. "What do you think of my ruby then? Is my jewel a good one?"

George put down his knife and fork with a small sigh and peered at Rose's ring with half closed eyes. She took it off and handed it to him.

"Well, it certainly looks like a genuine stone on first viewing," he said, holding it up to the light and watching the light bounce off the facets. "A very nice piece indeed and worth a small fortune I would say. Where did you get it from?"

"It came down through Mother's family and she gave it to me a few years back. I love it."

"Look after it well and make sure you have it insured." George handed the ring back and picked up his knife and fork again. "If you would like a professional valuation I would be happy to do so for you," he continued politely.

"I have some wonderful jewellery with me." Florence's voice rang out across the table. "Perhaps you could take a look at it for me some time?"

Catching Cordelia's eye for a second, George glanced across at Florence and reluctantly smiled in assent.

Once dinner was safely over, there seemed to be a collective sigh of relief. Walter stood up, cleared his throat, and tapped his glass with a small silver teaspoon. The tinkling rang out and everyone turned to face him.

"This is the time when the women would usually leave us and retreat to the drawing room while we men made our way to the smoking room, but tonight I would like to show you the end result of my latest project. It's something I am very proud of and have spent an enormous amount of money on."

An excited murmur sounded throughout the room.

"Let me lead the way." He strutted to the door like a little peacock spreading its tail out in all its colourful splendour. Grabbing the handle and opening it with force he ushered them all out into the hall. "Come this way please ladies and gentlemen."

Flinging open the front door, Walter cleared his throat yet again and tripped lightly out over the threshold leading the way down the steps onto the front lawn. He stood and waited next to a life-size statue of a Grecian goddess crowned with a crested helm and armed with a spear and shield.

Florence, chattering in nervous excitement and not worrying about having come outside, without her fur, followed closely behind. She didn't want to wear it in front of Cordelia anyway, as it was infinitely inferior to hers.

"Oh, is that meant to be Athena?" Hattie walked down the steps and looked at the statue and then at Harry who had come out behind her.

"It is," he replied with a grin. "She's usually accompanied by an owl, her sacred animal, but the poor creature got knocked off when it was being transported here. Father was livid!"

Hattie stifled a little giggle not wanting to be rude to her host.

Once outside, everyone marched down the path to the boathouse by the lake behind Walter. Opening the door with pride, Walter revealed the interior of the boathouse, which was clean but a little damp. A few colourful rowing boats bobbed about on the water and strained at the ropes that tethered them to the side. He swiftly crossed the room by way of a little wooden platform and opened a door that was partially hidden by a large potted rubber plant. Beyond it there was a spiral staircase leading down to a narrow stone passage, which disappeared underneath the lake at quite a steep angle and had an arched roof. No more than two people could walk side by side in it.

Walter went first, gazing in fascination at the stone walled passage surrounding him. It never ceased to impress him. Florence and Joseph went next, gazing in wonder around them and marvelling at the lighting, as they still had gas lamps at home. George walked behind them, hands in his pockets, gazing around in half suppressed fascination. Cordelia and Hattie went next, followed by Aubrey and Blanche and then Rose and Harry.

The passage wound on down and the guests went quiet, in awe at the engineering that must have gone into such a project. Could they really be walking under the water?

"I can't quite get my bearings right?" said Aubrey, and his voice echoed around them, bouncing off the walls and disappearing up the passage.

"We're quite a way under the lake," said Blanche. "It shouldn't be long before we reach the folly now. It's around 400 feet from the boathouse. If you remember where the statue was that you saw from the window earlier, we're just about there now."

Suddenly Walter stopped and called out to everyone. "Here we are. Be prepared for a surprise!" His voice took on a surreal echoing quality as it filtered back. He turned the key in the lock and flung open the door at the end of the passage shepherding everyone inside.

"Oooh, it's dark in here!" squealed Florence, grabbing hold of Joseph's arm. It was pitch black, and they all gathered in a huddle, straining their eyes to try and focus on something tangible.

Not being able to see anything properly apart from moving shadows, Joseph stumbled into Walter. "Sorry sir but I can't see anything. Should I sit down or do you receive your visitors standing up? If you preferred it I could curtsy and kiss your proffered hand."

"Don't be silly, Joseph," said Florence, detecting annoyance from a silent Walter.

There was a click as Walter triumphantly thrust the light switch down and, all at once, the room was flooded with light. The guests gasped and gazed around in amazement, blinking rapidly while their eyes adjusted.

The room was large and circular with an enormous rug in the centre. A chaise longue and several comfortable wing back chairs were dotted around, and potted palms stood to attention as if they were soldiers guarding something infinitely precious. A collection of guns hung in a glass cabinet to the left of the door. From the top of the roof right down to the floor, the room was a framework of metal with clear glass windows, much like the new conservatory in the house. Silver ashtrays and pretty lamps adorned the various tables that nestled between the chairs and a large tray of bottled drinks and stylish coloured glasses perched on a sideboard next to a gramophone and some records. Everyone could see that no expense had been spared.

The guests turned around, murmuring in surprise and delight at Walter's underwater room. Looking up, they took in the detailing of the arched glass roof above, watching the watery shapes creating moving shadows all around them.

"Mesmerising," said George in a low voice. The others murmured in agreement.

Walter turned on another switch and the roof was suddenly illuminated, giving a better view of the dark waters above. The colossal cherub statue that sat on the top of the folly roof seemed to frown down at them through the glass. It certainly didn't look as if it was that big when viewing it from the house. Cordelia shivered involuntarily.

It was a few seconds before anyone could speak, then Hattie said, "Mr Sinnet, I can't believe this room! It's incredible. My father was one of the labourers involved in creating the folly, but I never imagined it would be quite like this."

Walter beamed at her, basking in the sure-fire knowledge that he was being looked upon as the genius he already believed he was.

"Your father was involved? Well, how nice for you to see the fruits of his labours. Do tell him it was worth all the hard work when you go back home. You know it took more than two hundred men to dig and fill the lake and build this folly. It was a huge project to take on but I think you'll all agree that it was worth it? Anyway, all of you sit down, do." Walter gestured generously around him at the chairs. "I'll get us all some drinks."

He swaggered over to the sideboard drinking in the silence and perceiving it as adoration. The others sank into the deep luxurious chairs and continued to gaze up at the domed roof in silence. Fronds of greenery that had floated up from the plants at the bottom of the lake swished against the glass.

"How high is this room, Walter?" asked Florence gazing upwards. "I feel like I'm in a chapel."

"Around thirty-feet high."

"It's incredible; like a beautiful underwater conservatory. I can hardly take it all in."

"It's like there's a curtain of green water out there," said Joseph going over to one of the windows and pressing his nose up against it. "What will we see if we open them up?"

"Pass these drinks around Rose," Walter barked across at his daughter. Rose crossed the room frowningly, picked up the tray of brandy, and passed the drinks round to everyone except Hattie, who dismissed the tray with a slight shake of her head. She wasn't a great drinker and was unused to so much alcohol.

"Extremely impressive Walter," enthused Joseph. "I can't believe we are actually under the lake."

"Is that a fish swimming by?" asked Florence in excitement looking up at a dark shape moving fluidly across the top of one of the domed windows. "Oh look, there's another one! It looks like a kaleidoscope with all those changing colours and shapes."

"We must come and look in the daytime," said Joseph. "Everything is in shadow at night and I bet it's even more wonderful with the sunlight filtering down through the water. Do you have a lot of fish in the lake, Walter?"

"Yes I do," replied Walter, positively preening himself with self-importance. "I had them imported over here and then released into the lake by professionals. It has taken quite a while for them to become acclimatised to the water here. There's a breeding programme in place for them, so I'm hopeful they will increase in number over time."

"Will they be for fishing practice?" asked Aubrey wryly.

"Certainly not," replied Walter looking annoyed. "They are hugely expensive fish and no one will be allowed near the lake with a fishing rod I'm afraid. All of these windows are to serve as an aquarium so we can simply watch and enjoy them."

"Will this room just be for smoking and watching fish then?" asked Joseph.

"Predominantly yes," answered Walter looking irked. "Isn't that enough? However, I am thinking of putting a billiard table in here too for those that can't just sit and be."

"I didn't mean to cause any offence," gibbered Joseph guiltily. "I'm really impressed with this place. How could I not be? It's incredible."

Rose picked up the top record on the pile, removed it from its sleeve, and put it on the gramophone. "I like to come here to listen to music. Come on everyone, let's have a dance."

"I hope you're putting on Handel's Water Music," snorted Joseph.

Walter frowned as the music started to play and Rose began dancing on her own in the middle of the room holding her brandy glass.

Harry, noticing his father's face, grabbed Hattie by the hand and danced her across the rug, hoping to deflect attention from Rose.

Florence nudged Joseph, and he took the hint and also started to dance, albeit badly. Florence winced as he trod on her toes but smiled through it. "Walter looks cross with Rose," she said in his ear. "I hope he gets over it quickly. They say blood's thicker than water."

"Ah, but is blood thicker than Walter?" guffawed Joseph, capering about.

"Walter?" Blanche smiled at her husband and offered him her hand, but he turned his back on her and refilled his glass, his shoulders hunched and unfriendly. Blanche's smile disappeared off her face and was replaced by a sad expression until Aubrey came over and offered her his arm. She smiled up at him, took his arm and they began to dance. George remained seated, looking awkward and embarrassed. Dancing was not his forte.

"I only hope this folly is safe," said Cordelia to Walter, smirking, and watching the dancers laughing and spinning each other around. "We wouldn't want to end up swimming and dancing in cold water at this time of night. There must be tonnes of it pressed down on top of the roof."

"Of course it's safe," bristled Walter as he saw nervous glances pass between Joseph and Florence as they fox-trotted past. "We may be under water but this structure is amazingly safe. The engineer I used is world class, and I went through all the stages with him to make sure no stone was left unturned. Each pane of glass is three-inches thick."

"You're happy with your creation then?"

"Well, the passageway is slightly damp, but that's no surprise as it leads off from the boathouse. That is the only thing that irks. Oh, that reminds me, I need to get the butler to oil the door hinges. They're slightly squeaky. Anyway, no one will come to any harm here. I guarantee it." He raised his glass at the room in general and downed the contents in one gulp.

Chapter 4

The next morning brought driving rain and a wind that whistled down the chimneys and blew the petals off the roses in the formal rose garden. Florence shivered as she looked out of the bedroom window at the water being whipped up across the lake. Pericles was chasing the leaves and his fur was all ruffled up.

"I think we'll be staying indoors today Joseph. That storm is most definitely coming our way." She pulled her shawl round her shoulders and held it tight.

"Sounds good to me, old girl," replied Joseph, joining her at the window. "I need to get Walter on his own at some point to talk about that investment. To be honest if I don't get involved soon, we may be in some financial trouble. Don't want to end up in the poor house."

"Poor house? Don't joke about it, Joseph." Florence huffily turned away from the window and made her way to the door.

"Who's joking?" muttered Joseph under his breath and followed her downstairs to breakfast.

Hattie and Cordelia were sitting together in the morning room while Blanche went through the day's menu with Gladys.

"What dreadful rain. So glad we don't have to go outside." Cordelia had never been one for small talk and thought she would leave the room as soon as politeness allowed.

"Yes me too. I don't suppose you get weather like this in America?"

"No, in actual fact where I live it's usually too hot."

"I hear Mrs Sinnet often has the most wonderful fundraising fetes on the lawn so I'm thankful she didn't arrange one this weekend." Hattie, feeling a bit intimidated by Cordelia, was also planning to leave the room at the first opportunity. A silence drifted between them for a few seconds and then she continued. "What did you think of the folly?"

"It's a gorgeous vulgarity! Last night was the first time I'd seen it, as I wasn't really in the mood to view it before. You have to hand it to Walter with his strange ideas and architectural eccentricities; he's staggeringly ambitious. What did you think of it?"

"Personally I think it's wonderful, although I didn't think I would find it so. Despite all the labour from the men in the village and the money it brought to the families, there are still local concerns regarding the natural landscape. Mr Sinnet destroyed a lot of farmland to create the lake, and he allegedly has plans for another one."

"So I hear. Aunt Blanche told me he had originally decided to create a vast subterranean ballroom and further viewing conservatory and connect it to the smoking room via a series of passages. He changed his mind though, which I think is very sensible. There's no need for such ostentatiousness in my opinion."

"I hadn't heard that," said Hattie looking serious. "It doesn't sound as if it would be quite safe, all those passages and tonnes of water on top waiting to come flooding in." She shivered. "I'm not really the greatest fan of large bodies of water to be honest."

"You're the opposite of Walter then. I think he must be a little obsessed with lakes. He has three on the estate already."

"Three? My goodness, where are the other two?"

"One is on top of one of the hills to the far right, and the other is a few feet below it."

"Really?"

"Yes, really, and that's not the half of it. From the bathing pool, water pours through a magnificent marble statue of a dolphin's head into the lake you can see out there." Cordelia pointed vaguely towards the window.

"I'm almost sorry it isn't bathing weather outside," said Hattie. "However, it sounds a little frightening to me; I'm not used to such things. You can't see it from the house can you?"

"No, it's a bit of a walk to get there. I take it you haven't been here before then?" Cordelia was absent-mindedly twisting her wedding ring around her finger.

was over he would begin, he felt inspired. Smiling, his thoughts turned to the guests. There seemed to be a lot of tensions flying about already and it was only the first morning. It was typical of his parents to invite people who were completely different to each other and more than likely never to want to meet again. Jo and Flo were certainly on edge. He'd just seen Jo striding past him with a look of infinite worry etched across his brow. He didn't even notice when Harry had called out to him. Cordelia was hardly talking to anyone and looked pale. Rose was angry with Father again. Still, he couldn't blame her with the poor way she was being talked to at the moment. He seemed worse than usual. His thoughts flickered to the will change and then flickered away again. He wasn't going to worry about that now. George seemed reserved but that could just be his character, of course. Aubrey wasn't tense but then again he only seemed to have eyes for his mother. His thoughts turned to Hattie and a smile crossed his face. What a lovely girl, well read too. He'd show her the library later and lend her any books she fancied. Golly, he must like her, because he'd never allowed his books to leave the house before.

Harry was pulled up out of his musings by shouting in the study next door. He could hear his father's raised voice and another man's voice. What on earth was going on now? He crossed the library to the door and opened it in time to see George leaving the study wearing a grim expression. Joseph stood outside with his hand still raised as if about to knock on the door, surprise written all over his face.

"What was all that about?" Harry and Joseph stood uncertainly in the hall not quite knowing what to do when Walter opened the door. His angry look was rapidly replaced with one of forced jocularity when he saw the men. "Well, well, what have we here?" he blustered.

"I, er… we heard shouting sir," exclaimed Joseph.

"Is everything alright Father?" Harry watched his father closely.

"Yes, everything is fine. There's nothing for you to worry yourselves about. Business, that's all, it never runs smoothly. Did you want to see me, Joseph? Come in my boy." He moved back into the study, coughing and banging his chest with a clenched fist. Joseph followed him in and shut the door. Harry stood for a few seconds, looking concerned.

Luncheon, though delicious, was a strained affair and everyone seemed glad when it ended. They all seemed to be avoiding each other's eyes and Walter continuously snapped at Rose while she wore a thunderous expression on her pretty face. At long last the women retired to the drawing room to play baccarat, and the men donned galoshes to make their way to the smoking room. Luck was on their side and a gap in the weather brought a brief, pale watery sunlight to the garden as they made their way across the driveway and round the side of the house to the boathouse.

Walter switched on the lights, which flickered slightly as the wind picked up again, and they walked down the spiral staircase into the winding passage leading to the folly below.

Once inside, Joseph dropped into a chair and began to build his pipe with a shaking hand. His face was pale, and he looked upset. Walter had been adamant that the investment was off without even explaining the reasons to him properly. He had just said he couldn't help him and that was that, even when pleaded with. How could he be so callous? Did he want him to beg? Surely he had done something similar to his father in the past, now he came to think of it? He wracked his brains trying to remember, but it was all a bit hazy. He had a vague feeling that it wasn't all on the level and decided to ask his father on his return from his business trip what it had all been about. Joseph, hunched up in his chair, speculated on what he should do in the meantime.

George passed drinks around, looking much more at ease than he had before, almost as if he was a different person to the one they had met last night. His demeanour had definitely changed, and he seemed altogether too sure of himself all of a sudden. Walter, looking upwards at the glass roof and occasionally coughing, was quiet and reflective, his thoughts far away from his guests. His pompous attitude of earlier had disappeared.

The rain began to fall in torrents again, sweeping across the lake and making monstrous shadows on the walls of the folly. Despite the lamps it suddenly appeared altogether too dark. Harry shivered involuntarily as he sat down next to Aubrey and tried to start a light-hearted conversation with him about his planned book. Aubrey looked like he was listening, and nodded every now and again, but his face had a faraway expression on it. A sense of foreboding filled the room and the atmosphere became thick with menace.

One by one they made their excuses and went back to the house.

Chapter 6

Back in the drawing room, Rose was talking to Hattie about Harry. "I'm biased, I know, but he's the nicest man in the world. He's honourable and kind-hearted and nothing like Father!"

"A bit of a charmer too," said Hattie shyly, deliberately ignoring the remark about her host.

"It's about time he settled down. He could do with a nice wife, someone to share his passion of history and reading. He also keeps promising to write a book. The perfect woman would be able to type up his notes for him," she said mischievously. Hattie reddened and hastily changed the subject by asking Rose if she was planning on getting married.

"I guess I will one day, although not for a long time, as I wouldn't like to leave Mother all alone with Father."

"But she's not alone. What about Harry?"

"Harry? He'll be married within a year, you'll see!"

Cordelia seemed to have cheered up a bit and was trying to tempt the others to a game of indoor croquet instead of baccarat, but no one seemed that enthusiastic. The storm seemed to be worsening, and the wind began to whistle around the house in earnest. A crash came from somewhere and there was the distant sound of breaking glass.

"Oh dear, that sounds like we have a shattered windowpane," winced Blanche. "All these broken branches flying about the garden are going to do untold damage. I've never seen such a storm here before." She went off to find Gladys to investigate, with her.

No one showed any disappointment that dinner wasn't a social affair that evening. Joseph cried off with a headache, and Florence professed to not being hungry and stayed in her bedroom. Cordelia had been out for a short walk to get some fresh air and had got soaked in the rain. Thankful for modern plumbing she went upstairs to have a hot bath.

Only Aubrey, Blanche, Rose, Harry, and Hattie sat down to eat together. Hattie had timidly knocked on the door of the library to fetch Harry and, after a quick look around at the wall-to-wall shelves of leather-bound first editions, they wandered in to the dining room together talking animatedly. Neither George nor Walter appeared at all.

"There was a terrible mess in the conservatory," Blanche was saying. "Glass all over the floor and the chesterfields. Some of Walter's plants have had it I'm afraid. That glass will need to be fixed as soon as possible as all the heat is escaping, and the tropical ones will die off pretty quickly with this cold wind blowing about. Let's hope we don't have any other breakages before this storm has finished."

"What caused the glass to break?" asked Harry holding Hattie's chair out for her to sit down.

"I thought it was a branch, but it was actually a few tiles falling off the roof. The wind must have flung them down with some force."

"I detected a few smashed on the terrace as well," said Aubrey. "It may be prudent to get some buckets put up in the attic to prevent any rainwater leaking in and causing further damage."

"Good idea, Aubrey, and well spotted," said Harry getting up. "I'll go and talk to the servants now before I eat." He was back in a few minutes. "They've done it already, thankfully. It wouldn't be much fun to have water pouring through the ceilings onto our beds in the middle of the night. I must remember to go up and check them later."

"Mother," said Rose, remembering something. "I noticed you outside earlier calling the cat. Did he come in? I'd hate him to be stuck outside somewhere in this weather."

"He came running the second I called," laughed Blanche. "Greedy little thing thought he was getting a double dinner!"

"Well, I must say I rather like this smaller more intimate group," said Harry. He raised his glass and smiled down at Hattie. "Everything seems rather too tense for my liking today."

"I know what you mean," blushed Hattie. "I don't want to seem ungrateful or anything as I'm very happy to have been asked here, but something is up. There seem to be strange tensions going on under the surface."

"You're not wrong," said Rose putting her glass on the table. "I feel more than a little on edge myself for some reason."

"Well whatever it is, let's ignore it," suggested Aubrey. He began to recount an amusing anecdote about him and Blanche getting caught stealing apples when they were younger, and soon the whole table was laughing.

"I never got up to mischief like you two," giggled Hattie. "What naughty children you appear to have been! I'm afraid I always did what I was told and was the model child. How terribly dull I must have been."

"Rose was a bit of a mischief," laughed Blanche. "Harry was always in the library, even as a young boy and we had to practically drag him out for his meals. He was obsessed with books then and even more so now. Rose, however, spent her childhood with muddy knees and an impish spirit…always up to something or other!"

"Looks like you took after Mother then," said Harry grinning across the table at his sister.

"Well maybe you took after Father then," replied Rose with a glint in her eye and laughed out loud at Harry's horrified face.

"Perhaps you'll settle down and behave when you get married," said Aubrey looking at Rose fondly, almost as if he was her father.

"You never know! Anyway, why have you never married, Aubrey?"

"Rose," said her mother in mock shock. "You can't ask a question like that!"

"That's okay," laughed Aubrey. "I love your daughter's directness! How could I consider marrying anyone when the only woman I loved had already been taken?" He winked at Blanche.

"Maybe you will marry her one day," said Rose in a serious voice.

The wind raged on.

Chapter 7

Hattie sat bolt upright in bed, clutching her sheet to her chest. What on earth had woken her up? The curtains billowed into the room creating shadows of hellion proportions against the wall making Hattie shudder with fear. A flash of bright light illuminated the room for a second, followed by a prolonged clap of thunder. Hattie shivered and disappeared back under the covers squeezing her eyes tightly shut and putting her hands over her ears.

A haunting groaning sound came from outside between the wild sounds of the wind rushing back and forth across the garden and was followed by an almighty crash and the sound of metal squealing. Hattie's hair stood on end. A few seconds later she realised what it was. A tree, and a large one at that by the sound of it, had fallen down on the grand gates in the driveway. Oh goodness, what if one fell onto the house? She longed for her own bed and wondered how her mother was coping, alone in their little cottage.

"I shouldn't have come here," she murmured to herself. "If only this night were over."

She tried to make herself go back to sleep but there was a scratching sound coming from outside her bedroom door. What on earth could that be? The scratching stopped then started up again. It must be the cat wanting someone to protect it from the storm. Hattie, scared though she was, had a soft heart, and loved animals and she forced herself to get out of bed and crossed to the door.

"Pericles," she called softly through the keyhole and was pleased to hear a small mew outside. She opened the door a few inches and the little cat ran in purring and jumped onto Hattie's bed. She closed the bedroom door, happy to have the cat with her, and ignored the footsteps she could hear hurrying across the corridor. With Pericles cuddled up with her Hattie felt comforted and her nagging feeling of fear soon disappeared. She dropped off to sleep all of a sudden.

Harry, who had fallen asleep in front of the fire in the library, was woken up by the sound of a door banging and the storm battering against the house. The embers still glowed orange in the grate and lit up brightly as the wind blew down the chimney. Everything else in the room remained in shadow and Harry shivered. Yawning, he got up out of his comfortable chair and stretched. He placed the fireguard in front of the fireplace and peered out of the window through the half closed curtains. All was dark but he could make out the outline of the Athenian statue lit up by the lightning strikes, and saw shadows of leaves as they flitted back and forth across the lawn. It must be time for bed.

Harry padded over to the door and opened it quietly. There was no light at all and he felt his way gingerly across the hall to the staircase. As he began to climb slowly upwards, his back against the wall, another flash of lightning burst across the night sky and lit up a figure. The person appeared to be creeping stealthily across the landing towards the bedrooms.

"Who's that? Is everything alright?" Harry called out, but he heard the sound of footsteps running away down the corridor against the boom of the receding thunder.

Florence was shivering in her bed, half from fright, and half from cold. The fire had burned itself out, and the room was dark. "Joseph, are you awake?" she called across the room. No movement came from Joseph's bed. "I think a tree has come down. Did you hear that terrific crash?"

Supposing he must be sleeping very deeply, Florence huddled back under the covers and tried to get back to sleep.

George was enjoying being warm in his bed with the sounds of the howling wind outside. He loved a good storm. This one was tame in comparison to the ones he had witnessed in America though. He stretched his arms up out of the blanket and linked his fingers together behind his head, sighing contentedly. There was probably not going to be much sleep to be had tonight so he may as well lie back and enjoy the show. He thought he saw the shadow of his door opening against the wall but was too lazy to get up to shut it. The wind would only blow it open again anyway. He turned over on his side, shut his eyes, and saw the lightning flashes through his closed eyelids.

Cordelia was not having the same enjoyment as George. She hated storms and felt tired, emotional, and drained of all energy. If only she could drop off. A few good hours of deep comforting sleep would do her the world of good but it didn't look as if this would happen tonight. Although she had arrived at Witton Park a few days ago now, the trip from America had been long and arduous and had been steeped in stress. She cuddled down deep in the bed and pulled the sheet over her head. If only she could just go home and forget about everything.

Rose, who had slipped out of bed at the first echoing boom of thunder, rushed into her mother's room. She jumped into bed, as she had done as a child, and snuggled up to a yawning Blanche.

"Rose," laughed her mother. "You haven't got into bed with me since you were around ten years old!"

Rose laughed too. "Well, Mother, I'm only here because I thought you might not like the storm. Father's hardly a comfort is he?"

She peered over the top of the sheet and squinted across the room at her father's bed. "Why, he isn't even there! Where is he Mother?"

"I've no idea, dear. Sulking somewhere I expect!"

They chatted for a few minutes, watching the reflection of the lightning in the mirror on the dressing table opposite them, until Blanche started yawning again.

"I'll leave you in peace now. Good night Mother, sleep well." Rose blew a kiss at her mother and went back to her own room to try and sleep, but it eluded her for a long time.

The wind began to moan down the chimneys and a few more tiles came loose, clattered across the roof and smashed on the ground below. There was a sudden stillness as if the storm was taking a breath before its next onslaught. A few seconds later it seemed to gather itself together and began to target all of its energies at the front door. The door rattled violently in its frame and then suddenly crashed open, the hinges coming loose, and the wood around the frame splintering. The wind was relentless. It stormed in like a whirlwind and knocked two plants off the marble plinths in the hall and they came crashing down to the floor, the pots smashing into tiny fragments. The rain followed closely behind, soaking the floor and making it slippery.

Harry got out of bed, having only just got into it, and rushed down the stairs to see what had happened. He was closely followed by Aubrey who hadn't even gone to bed yet, but had been sitting by his bedroom window watching the lightning split the sky in two with every strike.

"Oh my goodness, look at the state of the front door. We need to find something to barricade it shut," said Harry in a loud voice that was shaking with concern.

"What have you got that's heavy enough?" shouted Aubrey above the rising scream of the storm.

"I'm not sure, perhaps the oak table?"

George appeared at the top of the stairs. "What's happening down there? Do you need any help?"

"Quick George, come and help us bring the oak table out of the dining room to lean against the front door."

The three men half carried, half dragged the heavy table out into the hall with some difficulty and Harry shut the door by leaning all his weight against it. Aubrey and George pushed the table in place and they sat on it sighing with relief.

"Thank you for helping," said Harry running his hand through his hair and looking at the mess in the windswept hall. "Did you hear the tree come down outside? I think it's crushed the gates, Father will be really angry. Anyway, I'd better go and clear up the plants that have crashed down here, as there's dirt everywhere. You two go and try to get some sleep. What a night." He picked his way across the hall and went in search of a dustpan, mop, and bucket.

"To be honest, I don't feel like going to bed now," said Aubrey and George nodded in agreement. "I may sneak into the kitchen and have a drink of hot milk, maybe with a small tot of whisky in it!"

"I think I'll join you and I may also get a snack. I missed dinner earlier and am suddenly feeling rather hungry." The two of them disappeared off in the direction of the kitchen.

The next morning eventually dawned. The storm had practically blown itself out, but it was still drizzly, blustery, and miserable outside. The wind had left a trail of destruction in the garden, but a watery sun was trying to make an appearance behind the grey clouds.

Chapter 8

As everyone was preparing to go down for breakfast, a scream rang out from one of the bedrooms.

"My jewellery! It's gone. Gone I tell you." George and Cordelia, who were making their way sleepily downstairs, turned around and hurried back across the landing. Harry was there already and tapped on the door. They could hear Florence wailing inside. Joseph flung open the door and beckoned them in; worry lines etched across his face. Florence was slumped dejectedly on her bed, empty jewel cases surrounding her. She looked up as they entered.

"I knew I should have got Gladys to put them in the safe yesterday. I simply knew it," she wept. "What are we to do?"

Blanche, Aubrey, Rose, and Hattie were sitting in the dining room, minus the table, eating a simple breakfast of devilled kidneys and bacon on plates balanced on their laps, with scalding hot tea perched on saucers on the floor by their feet. They could have eaten in the breakfast room, but were enjoying the informality of their picnic meal.

"I don't understand where your father got to last night," Blanche was saying to Rose. "He didn't turn up to supper, and he didn't come to bed. Well, if he did, he got up and disappeared again very early. Typical of him when we have guests here, disappearing off in his own world. It's very rude and embarrassing for me."

"You know what Father's like when it comes to business. He goes off for hours on end, guests, or no guests. He must have been worrying about something or other as he was going on about needing to see Mr Marlin. Anyway, I expect he's working on some important venture or other."

"Not with me, he's not," interrupted Joseph appearing at the door looking pale and exhausted. "He turned me down flat yesterday, despite promising great things. On top of that, the old girl's jewels have taken a walk." He collapsed into the nearest chair, putting his hands in front of his face.

"They've disappeared?" Blanche got to her feet. "Disappeared where? There must be some mistake. How could they simply not be where she left them? She said she was going to get them put in the safe, did she forget she'd done that?"

Aubrey wiped his mouth with his napkin, placed it on his plate, and then got up from his chair. He came and stood behind Joseph, tentatively putting a large hand on his shoulder.

"Why don't you tell us what happened old chap?"

"I can tell you that," said Florence in a loud voice, appearing at the door with George, Cordelia, and Harry. She sat down heavily next to Joseph and turned a tear-stained face up to them.

"I showed George my jewellery yesterday. It was all laid out in the morning room and he said the whole lot were fakes." She shot an angry look at George. "I was going to get Gladys to put it all in the safe, but I couldn't find her, so I took my precious jewels upstairs and hid them at the bottom of the wardrobe. I went to put on my diamond ring this morning and found that it was gone, along with everything else."

Rose inadvertently touched her ruby ring to make sure she was still wearing it and found to her relief that she was.

"Gladys must have taken it out for you and put it in the safe," said Blanche to Florence, going to the door. "I'll go and ask her." She returned five minutes later, looking worried. "Gladys hasn't touched it. Are you sure you didn't put it somewhere else?"

"Of course I'm sure! Why would I move it, and where would I put it?" Florence's voice got louder. She was on the edge of hysteria. "I want the house searched immediately."

"Where's Father?" asked Harry getting up. "He'll know what to do. I suppose he's in the study. Strange that he didn't come asking questions about the dining room table being shoved in front of the front door."

He went out of the room, crossed the hall, and rapped smartly at the study door. No answer, so he rapped again and then turned the handle. The door opened and Harry entered the room, but it was empty and no fire had been lit in the grate. He then went into the library, which was also empty. Where was he? He glanced into all the rooms on the ground floor, but Walter wasn't in any of them.

"Did you try the conservatory?" asked Blanche to her son. "I expect he's lamenting the loss of his plants."

"I looked in there already Mother but he wasn't there."

"In that case he must be in the folly," said Aubrey. "Shall I go and fetch him?"

"Oh yes please Aubrey. That would be helpful." Blanche sat down and gave a sigh as Aubrey left the room. Seconds later they saw him trotting down the drive towards the boathouse, oilskins flapping in the breeze, holding his hat on with one hand.

Rose was looking suspiciously at George who in turn was looking at Cordelia.

"Why don't we all take a seat and wait for Father?" Harry took charge. "Come on. There's nothing we can do until he arrives. Sit down do. The jewels aren't going to disappear from wherever they are at this second." Those who were still standing about sat down and a heavy silence hung over them.

Blanche got up again and bustled about, plumping cushions up and trying to make herself busy.

"George, would you help me move the table back in here please?" asked Harry. "I must find the tool box and try to fix the hinges on the front door."

George nodded in agreement and they left the room together, reappearing a few seconds later and straining under the weight of the oak table. Joseph got up and minced his way over to help. They pushed it back into place and put the chairs back where they belonged under it, and then Harry went in search of some tools. He wasn't gone long.

"It's okay," he said as cheerfully as he could. "The butler is going to fix it. The hinges are slightly bowed but nothing that can't be sorted out thankfully. The lock is fine too, so we won't need to find a locksmith. Jolly handy chap that man, shame he can't fix the iron gates too! They are completely mangled up under the weight of that tree."

A few minutes later Aubrey reappeared, shoulders wet from brushing past the rhododendrons on the path outside. "The folly is unlocked, but he's not there, and what's more, he can't have gone off the property, unless he went yesterday evening. A huge tree is down and is lying across the top of the driveway on top of the gates. The roots have been ripped right up out of the ground as it was so waterlogged. It's really quite something to see."

"I'm not worried about the gates, but I am worried about Walter. He had no reason to leave the property. Where is he?" Blanche turned worried eyes to Aubrey. "I must have a look upstairs. Does anyone have any objection to me peeping into the bedrooms? I don't believe he's in any of them, but I feel the need to check." Hearing no answer she briskly walked out of the room and everyone heard her feet click clacking down the hallway towards the stairs.

Harry stoked up the fire and stood looking into it, thinking hard, and was soon joined by Rose who said in a low voice, "Harry, what do we know about George? Did you see his face when Mother said she was going to peep in the bedrooms? Do you reckon he took the jewellery?"

"He might have taken it. One of us certainly must have." Harry continued to stare transfixed into the face of the fire as if hypnotised by it. "I'm not really sure what to do. If we start searching bedrooms it's going to put everyone's backs up, thinking they're being suspected of theft."

"We probably don't have much choice though, do we?"

"No, but when Father reappears and finds his guests up in arms about being accused of stealing the jewels he'll be livid."

Blanche soon returned looking puzzled. "Well, I have no idea what has happened to Walter. He's not in any of the bedrooms and I even had a quick look up in the loft, but I'm sure he will show up when he's good and ready." Her steady voice betrayed the emotion that was bubbling up inside her. "Don't worry my dear," she said to Florence. "Perhaps Walter hid the jewellery away for you to keep it safe, or was having some of the items professionally valued or something."

Florence opened her mouth to retort, but seeing a look from Joseph she shut it again. She knew Walter wouldn't steal into her room in the dead of night and remove her jewellery on the pretext of getting it valued. How would he know it was there in the first place?

The rest of the morning passed by quite quickly. The men disappeared down the drive with axes to see what they could do about removing the branches of the giant tree and the women sat around in the morning room. Blanche continued her embroidery, and the others sipped hot tea and tried to make small talk as if everything was normal. Only Florence was silent, occasionally glaring round at everyone in suspicion.

Joseph found the axe rather heavy and couldn't swing it very well. Every time he tried to chop at the tree trunk, he would send a shower of dirt over the others.

"Perhaps you should do something else, old boy?" suggested Aubrey as he wiped mud off his face for the umpteenth time.

Feeling relieved, but slightly embarrassed, Joseph bustled about picking up debris from the lawn and throwing it on the pit where the bonfire was usually made. He worked hard, making a large pile, and putting heavy branches on top to stop it all blowing away.

Eventually the lunch gong sounded, and the women filed through into the dining room to eat. The butler called the men and they went in at once, kicking off muddy shoes, and going to wash their hands and faces before joining the others. The food was exquisite, but no one seemed to taste it really and conversation floundered despite the best efforts of Aubrey and Blanche. Only Harry and Hattie seemed to enjoy it, chatting away about Greek gods. Florence raised her eyes up in annoyance.

"Of course, if you had to be one of the gods I'd put you down as Hermes," she heard Hattie saying playfully. "Bright, full of fun, and a mischievous grin!"

Harry laughed. "Well, young lady, I don't know you well yet but I like to think you would be like Bast. She was from Egypt, actually, not Greece but was a cat goddess and protected pregnant women and children. She loved music, dancing, and perfume."

"A cat goddess... well, I certainly have taken to Pericles so maybe it could be so!"

"Do you think the famous cat goddess would be able to locate my missing jewellery?" interrupted Florence rudely, her cheeks reddening in anger. Joseph patted her hand in a consolatory manner and she quietened down at once.

Gladys bustled in with a jam roly-poly and everyone began to eat it half-heartedly. Most of it was sent back to the kitchen much to cook's annoyance.

Chapter 9

When lunch was finally over, and everyone had enjoyed a strong cup of coffee, they trouped down to the folly to listen to the gramophone. Cordelia had suggested that they all needed to lighten the atmosphere and take some time out to wait for Walter to return from wherever he was.

Misty rain soaked the already sodden grass, but at least the air was refreshing. The path was thick with mud and the women picked their way over it holding their skirts up out of the way and trying to keep their hair from whipping across their faces.

Once inside, Rose and Cordelia flipped through the records and Aubrey fixed everyone a drink from the tray. George and Joseph lit pipes and Blanche wandered about the room nervously straightening already straight ashtrays on the tables. She closed the gun cabinet door that had swung half-open and sat down on the edge of one of the chairs. Harry and Hattie sat together talking in low voices while Florence jabbered on and on feverishly to anyone who would listen to her talk about her missing jewels.

All of a sudden the music rang out of the gramophone taking everyone by surprise. The piano filled the room with its sheer volume while the violins built up to a crescendo of sound, seeming to fill the whole place, making it claustrophobic and hard to breathe.

Hattie took a deep breath, and then another. She felt as if she wanted to run away and find a wide-open space where she could breathe properly and feel the warm sun on her skin.

Harry looked as if he could be struggling too. Was there even enough air in the folly? He stood up and walked a couple of times around the room before sitting back down again next to Hattie. They looked at each other with anxious expressions and tried to smile.

Joseph knocked his pipe out in one of the ashtrays. Although he'd only lit it a minute or two before, he couldn't find any enjoyment in it at all. George shrugged and continued to puff on his, studiously ignoring everyone. He wasn't enjoying his much either, but needed something to do with his hands. He gazed moodily at the table, feeling hypnotised by the watery shadows shrinking and swelling on the shiny surface.

As Aubrey switched on the lighting that lit up the domed roof, a scream rang out, going on and on, and getting louder by the second, matching the upsurge of the string section. It was Florence, and she was pointing up to the roof. It was then that everyone saw him. Walter. Facing down towards them, drowned and bloated, swaying in time to the music, along with the pondweed, across the outside of the glass. The weeds cast a green glow onto his face.

Time seemed to stand still for several seconds as everyone took the situation in, then Hattie turned and buried her face in Harry's chest. "Oh, I can't look. I can't look." Harry put his arms around her and held her close.

Blanche swayed and was caught by Aubrey as she fell into a dead faint. He picked her up as if she were as light as a feather and carried her to the chaise longue.

"Mother?" Rose dropped the gramophone record that she was holding, raced across the room, picked up her mother's hand, and held it to her cheek. "Mother, oh wake up do. Mother what are we to do?" She turned round wildly. "Does anyone have any smelling salts on them? How has this happened?"

Aubrey absent-mindedly patted her back in a gesture that was both fatherly and comforting.

The music reached its peak with an explosion of cymbals, and the kettledrum bellowed out its dramatic end.

George drained his whisky in one gulp and crossed over to the gramophone. He took the needle off the record and an eerie silence hung over the room at once.

Joseph, looking awful, had his head between his knees. Florence's screams had abated but she was still staring open-mouthed upwards with wide horrified eyes.

Cordelia went to the door and snapped the roof's light switch off and the image of Walter disappeared almost as if the curtain had gone down on the final act of a play. Hysteria rose up inside her and she felt almost as if she should be standing up and applauding.

Blanche was looking pale and she sat up, holding her lavender scented hanky to her nose. She looked at Rose and they searched each other's faces as if they would find some kind of an answer there. Harry gently extracted Hattie from him and sat her down on one of the chairs, then swiftly crossed the room to his sister and mother. They held on tightly to one another, disbelief coming over them in waves.

Time seemed to stand still until Aubrey, taking charge, decided that the women must get back to the house as soon as possible. As they all ascended shakily up the passage and out through the boathouse, a ground fog began to roll across the grass towards them and out over the lake. They hurried past the rhododendrons, Aubrey holding the longest branches back out of the way, and up the muddy drive, shivering and in shock.

Gathering together around the fire for warmth and comfort, Gladys brought in hot sweet tea, tears pouring down her face when she heard what had happened. She put the tray down and left the room, wiping her face with her apron and sniffing loudly.

"He must have fallen in some time yesterday," Blanche was saying. "We should have looked for him when he didn't come in for supper. How I can ever forgive myself I simply don't know."

"Come now Blanche," said Aubrey in a reassuring voice. "You couldn't have done anything. The poor chap must have lost his footing and that was that. The wind was terrible. You don't have a single thing to forgive yourself for."

"He wasn't a well man and I should have kept a closer eye on him."

"What do you mean by saying he wasn't well, Mother? He was perfectly fine," said Rose, visibly shaken. "The peak of fitness I'd say."

"I'm afraid he wasn't perfectly fine, my dear. His cough was bad and he frequently cleared his throat," replied Blanche. "A few months ago we were at a house party and one of the guests was a doctor. He heard the coughing and told Walter he had a nasty sounding chest and it sounded pretty serious to him. His guess was consumption and he told Walter to go and see him at his clinic for tests as soon as the weekend finished. Walter refused to go and insisted he was fine despite me pleading with him. He said the doctor only wanted his money, and was in total denial that there was anything wrong with him. I knew, though, that he really was in a bad way and I know that he knew it inside too."

"Mother, why didn't you tell us?" cried Harry aghast.

"I wanted to but he wouldn't let me. I think he realised that it would be the death of him one day. His cough became more and more frequent and his chest was painful inside. Despite everything, he wasn't a stupid man. I tried to persuade him to go for the tests but he just got cross with me for bringing it up. He must have had a funny turn and fallen into the lake and got into difficulties trying to get out. How terrifying for him. I hate to think of him frantically thrashing around in that cold water all alone."

"I'm sorry you carried that worry on your shoulders on your own," said Rose looking sad. "If only you had shared it with us. I know we couldn't have done anything to help, but a problem shared is a problem halved or so they say."

"Poor Father, I hope he didn't suffer too much." Harry looked melancholy. "Maybe that's why he was so annoyed at Mr Marlin cancelling his stay here this weekend. He must have wanted to get his affairs in order."

"He can't have known he was going to die this weekend," cried Rose.

"Perhaps not. Anyway, I'm going to go and telephone for the police." He tried to sound more cheerful than he felt for the sake of his mother and sister. "We'll soon have this all sorted out, don't worry. It is going to be hard, but we will cope without him, I'll make sure of it." He left the room swiftly.

"We haven't managed to shift that tree, although we've made major inroads into it," said Joseph. "There's no getting help up here in a hurry. What should we do?" He turned worried eyes on the group.

"Can't someone go through the fields that border the grounds?" asked Cordelia questioningly.

"No go I'm afraid. We had a look and the fields are completely waterlogged, like sinking sand. We'd wade right up to our middles... that's if we could even scale those walls to get into them."

Harry came back into the room looking concerned. "The telephone's dead. I'm sure it'll be sorted out soon though as the telephone exchange is always quick to sort out problems. I'll keep trying every half hour or so."

"Well, we must get him out of the lake ourselves then." Aubrey took a deep breath and continued. "I'll volunteer to go, but who's coming to help me? Not the women, of course."

"But Aubrey, you can't," breathed Blanche. "It's awful outside and it would not be fun going out in a boat in this weather."

"I'm certainly not expecting fun. I just don't think we should leave him there in the lake." Aubrey took her hand in his and gave it a small squeeze. "Where there's a will there's a way."

"Where there's a will there's a relative," quipped Joseph looking round to see who had found him funny.

"Hush Joseph, this is no time for tasteless jokes," said Florence prodding him with her finger.

Joseph subsided and bowed his head in mock embarrassment.

Chapter 10

Joseph decided to stay with the women as he said they needed a man with them, so George, Aubrey, and Harry set off down the drive together with set expressions on their faces, disappearing into the fog. At the boathouse they took boat hooks off the wall and placed them in the bottom of one of the rowing boats, then getting in, they pushed off and began to navigate their way towards where they imagined the cherub statue to be. It wasn't easy as the wind remained quite strong and kept blowing them off course.

"This is not right," said Harry after five minutes, straining his eyes to try and spot the cherub through the damp white clouds that surrounded them and clung to their clothes. "I'm sure we're too far to the left." The water lapped up against the side of the boat, tapping its icy fingers against the wood.

"You let us know where you think we should go and we'll follow your instructions," said Aubrey. "My goodness, this really is freak weather. In the space of two days we've had sun, rain, wind, thunder and lightning, and now fog." He picked up the oars again and began to row in the direction Harry was looking towards.

"I'm pretty sure it's this way."

The boat seemed to be turning round in circles and the wind was hard to row against. They drifted about, completely lost, their backs getting soaked as they hunched them against the dismal weather.

George squinted at the two men beside him and then wiped at the lenses of his glasses with his sleeve. "Damn this fog. I can't see a thing."

"Me neither," said Aubrey.

In the distance and getting nearer was the sound of roaring water, angry and relentless.

"Is that just the weather or the sound of a waterfall?" asked Aubrey in surprise. "I didn't know there was one on this side of the lake."

"Oh we're here are we? Yes Aubrey, there are a few waterfalls on this side, hidden in the inlet around the left side of the lake, beyond the tall trees," said Harry. "The lake has been made in such a way that it's what you would call split level, with large rocks built up so that the water pours over them. Father said it is engineering at its best, but I'm afraid it doesn't really do much for me. In fact it gives me the creeps. I never come over this side of the lake unless it's absolutely necessary."

"I can handle a few small waterfalls, but what on earth is that?" suddenly called out George, pointing with a trembling finger. They could hear the roar of water getting closer and through the patchy moving fog they could see an unreal scene set out before them. There were large moss-covered rocks with life-size white water nymphs sitting on them, with some rising up out of the water and looking as if they were engaged in an act of worship to some higher deity. Water poured over the rocks in smooth curtains that crashed into the lake causing foamy white waves below.

"These are Father's favourite statues. We've come the wrong way, but I can see where we've gone wrong now."

The boat drifted closer as Harry fiddled with his oar, and George felt every fibre of his being want to turn tail and get away as fast as possible, but the boat kept relentlessly moving forward. A patch of fog cleared, and they found themselves below two massive winged horses that were rearing up at least fifteen feet above them from the topmost rock. Neptune stood up with a foot on each horse, whip in hand and looking as if he was riding them out of the lake with all the power of the sea at his command. Aubrey found himself transfixed, despite his extreme reluctance to be as close as he was.

"Are these the statues that your father imported from Italy?" he asked Harry. "I heard that a road had to be lowered to fit one of them under the bridge but I didn't believe it."

"They are the ones from Italy but not the ones the road had to be lowered for," replied Harry in embarrassment. "You're thinking of the dolphin head statue. He had that one specially made and brought over by boat. The thing was so big that it wouldn't fit under the bridge near the port. Father was determined, though, and paid a vast sum to make sure it arrived here in one piece. As for these statues, Mother hates them and that is why they're hidden around this corner of trees."

Aubrey and George tried and failed to tear their eyes away from the spectacle before them, the sound of the waterfalls still roaring in their ears. At last, a thick curtain of fog clouded their view, shaking them out of their dream-like state.

"Are we likely to row into anything else out of the ordinary?" asked George hotly.

"No I don't think so now. I know where to go from here."

Having got his bearings, Harry pointed them in the right direction and they all began to row, slightly faster than they would have done before, hunched up against the cold wind.

Back in the warmth of the living room, Florence was sharing her misgivings about George. "It doesn't quite add up. He said my jewels were all fakes, and then they disappeared. It is all very suspicious if you ask me."

"He's not likely to have taken them if he'd known they were fakes," snapped Cordelia. "It's far more likely to have been someone who thought they were genuine."

"Well he could have said they were fakes, knowing that they weren't, to avert suspicion from him. What exactly do you know about him, Cordelia?"

"The same as you, Florence," drawled Cordelia crossing her legs and tapping her fingers on her knee.

"Well I'm not so sure. I saw you talking to him outside the night we arrived. Yet when you were introduced you acted as if you were meeting for the first time."

Cordelia looked put out for a second but soon came back with, "Why Florence, I never had you down as a peeping Tom."

Florence was about to retort when Joseph interrupted. "Come now ladies, let's not fall out. We've all had a nasty shock and need to support each other at this time."

"Yes, but it is a bit strange Cords you have to admit," said Rose, looking across at her cousin. "I'm glad I haven't taken my ruby off to be honest. Did you already know him?"

Cordelia glared at Rose, was silent for a while, and then sighed a long and heartfelt sigh. "Yes, alright, I suppose you'll keep nagging at me if I don't tell you. If you must know, we met in America and he is a genuine dealer in jewels. He knows what he's talking about."

"You *did* know him? Why keep it a secret then and why didn't you want us to know?"

Cordelia pursed her lips together and said nothing.

"What is this all about dear?" asked Blanche looking perplexed.

Cordelia got to her feet and went and stood by the mantelpiece, her back to the room. Suddenly she spun around. "All I will say is that I can tell you for certain that George did not take your rotten jewels. You have my personal guarantee on that."

Try as they might, no one could get another word out of her on the subject.

Aubrey, George, and Harry were finally nearing the centre of the lake having gone round in circles for what seemed like an interminable amount of time. The cherub seemed to loom towards them in a menacing fashion, the fog curling around its legs like a spider wrapping its prey in its web. Harry threw the rope to try to get it over one of the statue's feet, but it missed and thwacked on the surface of the water sending droplets of cold spray over them. He hauled it back out of the lake and tried again, this time ringing it over perfectly.

They pulled themselves along the rope, steadying the boat and stopped next to the bottom of the statue. It rose out of the water and pointed off into the distance as if warning them to get out of there quickly. George felt as if he'd seen enough statues to last him a lifetime and was regretting coming to Witton Park in the first place.

The bottom of the boat scraped against the glass of the folly roof as it stopped, making a muted screeching sound that echoed out across the lake mournfully. Harry shivered and pulled his coat more firmly around himself, holding it at the throat. He could hear his heart beating loudly and felt nausea rise up from deep within. Swallowing hard, he heard George say in a mock cheerful voice, "Right then, here we are. Let's try to get at him."

The three men peered down over the side of the boat trying to catch a glimpse of Walter, but the fog combined with the murky green of the floating vegetation made it impossible. Aubrey stood up and jabbed one of the boat hooks over the side and into the water, making Harry visibly wince. George followed suit, but a bit more gently. He put his hook in the water and began to move it about from side to side in the hope of catching onto Walter's clothes.

"Here he is. I think he has got caught on the rough base of the statue where it meets the roof." Aubrey jabbed again and tried to hook Walter's coat. "Come on, help me reach him."

The boat rocked violently, threatening to throw them all over the side.

"Careful! I think we need to steady ourselves and try one at a time. I really don't want to end up in the lake." George put his hook in again and managed to dislodge Walter from the statue. He began to float up to the surface, and Harry's pallor turned a greyish green. George hooked his shirt collar and said, "I have him. You two start to row and I'll hold on."

The boat cut a path across the water, the little waves rippling out in ever widening circles and the fog clung to Walter's clothes like a macabre spectre trying to pull him back to its lair.

"Hang on a moment chaps, my hands are so cold I can't hold on." George flexed his fingers to alleviate the cramp that was creeping up on him and Walter began to slip back under the surface of the lake. Aubrey reached over the back and grabbed hold of the disappearing jacket collar, nearly losing his oar from the rowlock. Harry made a lunge for it and the boat rocked wildly again.

"Let's just get back. I can't stomach much more," he said, trembling with cold and emotion. They began to row again, the oars cutting through the water like knives through melting butter, putting all of their combined efforts together to make the nightmare come to a rapid end.

An almost palpable silence accosted them as they glided the last few metres back into the dripping cavern of the boathouse, wet and exhausted, and climbed out of the boat shivering with horror. Dragging Walter out of the water, and narrowly avoiding toppling in themselves, they manhandled him down the spiral staircase with difficulty and then hurried along the underground passage to the folly, trying not to knock him into the walls on the way.

Harry opened the door, and they struggled in, panting, and put him down on the rug as gently as they could. Harry flicked the light switch on, making them blink in the sudden light, and tried not to look at his father lying there stone cold dead.

"What do we do now?" asked George. "I guess we should cover him up with something."

"Good idea. Do you have a rug down here at all, Harry?" asked Aubrey, patting Harry gingerly on the shoulder. "It would be far more respectful to leave him covered up."

Harry looked around and shook his head. "No, I don't think there's anything here. I could go back to the boathouse and get a tarpaulin off one of the boats. Will you come up and help me, George?"

"Yes, of course."

The two men began to walk to the door when Aubrey gave a gasp. "Look! He's been shot!"

Chapter 11

"Mother, will the gardeners be coming tomorrow? They simply have to move that tree. I feel claustrophobic!" Rose looked at her mother with wild eyes.

"Yes dear, they should be here tomorrow, weather permitting. It is their day to come after all. No one can leave anyway, not until the police have been." Blanche's pinched face looked out of the window and saw the grim expressions of the three men returning from their mission, shoulders hunched and heads bowed as they negotiated the sopping branches of the rhododendrons.

"It's fine to be here on a normal day, but knowing I can't leave when I want to is pure torture. Why do the police need to come? Surely we just need a doctor to come and sign a death certificate, and his body to be removed from the property?"

"They always have to come, my dear," replied Blanche patiently. "I wish the telephone was working because we need to inform Mr Marlin as soon as possible too. We shall need his help."

Hattie was weeping silently into her handkerchief and Florence was eyeing Cordelia in unsuppressed suspicion. They heard the sound of shoes tramping through the hall and Joseph stood up as the men came through the door into the room. "Right chaps, whisky is it?" He poured stiff measures into glasses and handed them around, watching them drain the amber coloured liquid quickly.

Gladys had brought thick blankets in and the men put them round their shoulders holding them close.

"What happened? Did you manage to get him out of the water?" asked Blanche.

Harry nodded, looking down at his feet, and not saying anything.

"It took a few attempts, but we managed to get him out. We put him in the folly," said George in a low voice.

"My dear, I hate to tell you this, but Walter was shot." Aubrey took Blanche's hands in his cold ones.

"Shot?" Blanche took her hands away from Aubrey's and took a few steps back. "What do you mean, shot? He can't have been. Who would... who would do such a thing?" She looked round at everyone in horror.

Rose's hands flew to her face. Hattie nervously pleated at the fabric on her skirt, and Florence swallowed once or twice. Joseph, open-mouthed and glad he hadn't gone out, looked stunned. Cordelia's face betrayed no emotion whatsoever.

"Did he take his own life?" asked Hattie turning a tear-streaked face towards Harry.

"No. Impossible I'm afraid; he was shot in the back." Harry sat down heavily on a chair, still clutching the blanket in tight fists.

It took a while to sink in. Not only had Walter died, which was bad enough, but one of them must have killed him. They began to look around at each other, questions sticking in their throats and being swallowed back down again before reaching their lips. No one knew what to do and time passed slowly as they sat about waiting for someone to do or say something constructive.

"Murder is gruesome at the best of times, and this is definitely not the best of times," murmured Joseph.

Harry eventually took charge. "I didn't expect to be saying this for many years yet, but I'm the man of the house now. I will tell you what we're going to do. We're going to get Gladys to bring in some food and we are going to eat something. We will not talk about this until we have finished. Things are sorted out easier on a full stomach."

"I couldn't eat a thing, Harry old boy," protested Joseph, and the others nodded in agreement but Harry was firm. He went out of the room to go and give instructions to the kitchen. He was feeling sick to the stomach but didn't know what else to do. He would force himself to eat. They had to continue in their normal routine.

A light dinner over, with the strain of splintered conversations about anything else but the situation in which they found themselves, everyone put down their napkins and Harry stood up to go and see if the telephone line was back in action. It wasn't, and he soon returned to them looking crestfallen.

"I hate to say this but the truth is that one of us is a cold-blooded murderer. One of us has taken my father's life, because no one could have come onto the property in this mad weather. The property is cut off and we are the only ones here."

"You're also forgetting that one of us has stolen my jewellery," interrupted Florence vehemently.

"Yes Florence we are fully aware of that," snapped Cordelia impatiently.

Harry held his hand up for silence. "Now, let's try and get to the bottom of it. Who was the last person to see him alive? That's my first question."

"Well it can't have been any of us women," offered Rose, getting up and standing next to her brother. "All of you men were with him in the folly and we were all together in the drawing room."

"Yes, that's true," said Harry thoughtfully. "When I left the folly, Joseph and George were still in there with Father. Aubrey left before me. I remember because I knew he wanted to get back to mother, to spend time with her." He looked at Blanche but she didn't quite meet his eyes, and turned away to look out of the window.

"Yes, I was the first to leave," said Aubrey without embarrassment, casting his mind back. "You were all still in there when I went out."

"Well I hope you're not accusing me," squeaked Joseph in a high voice. "I couldn't kill a spider, could I Florence? Besides, I left before George did." He looked at his wife appealingly.

"Of course it wasn't you, Joseph," Florence said looking at her husband in horror. "Anyway, you would have no reason to do so."

Hattie looked at Joseph, she wasn't so sure. He was upset that Walter did not want him to invest in his company and had told them all. He had been distraught. Harry seemed to read her mind and turned to Joseph. "The investment, Jo... Father turned you down with no reason. Remember?" Everyone eyed Joseph with a deep suspicion and he seemed to wither in front of their eyes.

"Well yes that's true, but I wouldn't murder him would I? That wouldn't keep me out of the poor house, it wouldn't solve anything." His monocle fell out and swung backwards and forwards on its chain. "I wouldn't. I couldn't."

The scales of belief seemed to flicker back over to Joseph's side as no one could see why he would do such a thing. Anyway, he had left the room before George, so he said.

All eyes turned to George, and he looked defiantly back at them.

"He was alive when I left him. I left shortly after Joseph as Walter and I had nothing to say to each other. I'm afraid murder isn't my game," he said in a low voice.

"Then what is?" Harry spoke with authority. "You may as well tell us, because no one will be leaving this place until we find some answers. One of us is going to hang, damn it. Don't let it be the wrong person simply because they wouldn't talk openly and honestly."

The wind began to pick up again and whistled down the chimney sending sparks from the fire across the hearth and making Pericles jump. Harry jabbed at the fire with the poker and it hissed as a few drops of rain came down with the wind.

Gladys bustled in with the butler and they drew the curtains across the windows as the sky began to darken outside. They bustled out again taking the remnants of the meal with them.

"Cords, I think you may know something about this. Please tell us," implored Rose, appealing to her cousin.

Cordelia remained defiantly silent, thrusting her chin out.

Rose sighed.

Hattie appealed to Harry. "Shall I write down all that is said, Harry? We will need notes, won't we? You just let me help, I need to feel useful."

Harry nodded at her and smiled gratefully into her eyes. "That'd be great, Hattie. I'll fetch a notepad from the library." He was back in seconds, handing it to her along with a pencil. "Do you have any idea where to start?"

"Well, I was wondering if any of us could remember what order and time the men returned to us after leaving the folly."

"Well I returned first, obviously, didn't I Blanche?" said Aubrey straightaway.

"Well, yes, I'm sure you did, if you say so," replied Blanche, her forehead wrinkling up in thought. "I really can't remember and I have no idea of the time either."

"You must remember, you old silly," laughed Aubrey. "We were trying to hide the indoor croquet set from Cordelia."

"Oh that's right," smiled Blanche. "We put it behind the curtains in the end! That seems like weeks ago."

Cordelia glowered at them.

Harry watched Hattie scribbling on the notepad and said, "I must have come in next. I went straight to the library. Again, I have no concept of what time it was."

"Well, we have no proof of that," burst out Florence. "You had a reason to bump Walter off as he wanted you in the firm but you refused. It's well known he threatened to remove you from his will if you didn't start pulling your weight and had even invited his solicitor here this weekend to change his will, or so he said at dinner!" she finished triumphantly.

"He was all bluster. He wouldn't have removed me really, and in any case, money doesn't interest me. But, of course, I'm a suspect much the same as anyone else. I can't prove I was in the library, but that's where I was, looking up a reference to an earlier conversation I had with Hattie about Zeus."

Hattie looked up.

"I remember going straight up to my room," interrupted Joseph. "My clothes were damp, and I wanted to change. No one saw me to my knowledge."

All eyes flickered towards George again.

Hattie gave a little cough. "Let's get things straight," she uttered in a small voice, looking at Harry for affirmation. "I have everyone's name down on this pad, including myself of course. I am going to write possible reasons for each one of us killing Mr Sinnet."

A log shifted in the grate making everyone jump slightly.

"You go for it, Miss Marple," chortled Joseph, and Florence nudged him.

Hattie's cheeks coloured and she continued in a shaky voice. "I've started with Aubrey, seeing as he was the first to leave the folly. He wanted Walter out of the picture so that he could marry Blanche."

"Of course I did," said Aubrey in a jovial kind of voice, winking at Blanche. "Everyone knows it, no secret there I'm afraid. It didn't happen though. I didn't kill the man."

Hattie blushed once again and looked down at the floor. "I'm afraid I overheard you telling Blanche you would kill him to marry her."

"Ah, so that was you, was it?" Aubrey's smile disappeared for a second.

"I didn't mean to eavesdrop. As soon as I heard you talking I shut the door and went away. I realised it was a private conversation."

"Don't worry, Hattie. You didn't do anything wrong. Please continue with your notes," said Blanche.

"Right." Hattie looked down at her notepad. "Harry..." she hesitated.

"It's fine, you can say it," smiled Harry.

"Harry could have wanted his father out of the way in order to inherit some money and not have to join the company. He had to do it before the solicitor came."

"You're right of course and I'm probably the most obvious suspect. However, I didn't shoot my father." A muscle in Harry's cheek was twitching. "Do carry on Hattie."

"Joseph was angry that Walter would not let him invest anything into the company despite being told he would be able to."

Joseph grimaced but remained silent.

"George is here on business and was overheard having an argument with Walter in the study. Perhaps Walter tried to con him in some way."

"Surely I wouldn't need to murder him unless he had actually got away with conning me," said George with an edge to his voice.

"Also, it seems he knew Cordelia before this weekend, but chose to keep quiet about it," continued Hattie avoiding George's eye.

"Sheer speculation," interrupted Cordelia with a grim look on her face.

Hattie continued talking. "I hope I'm not talking out of turn, Blanche, and I don't know if it's true or not, but people in the village say that Walter made his money by dishonest means. It could just be jealous gossip."

Blanche opened her mouth as if to protest and then shut it again. She gave a small nod.

"Florence has the same reason as Joseph. They needed the money and were let down."

"Well I hope to think that nobody could ever imagine that I could commit a violent act against a fellow human," sniffed Florence. She went and stood looking out of the window, her back to the room.

"Blanche may have wanted Walter out of the way so she could be happy with Aubrey." Hattie turned to look at Blanche. "Even I noticed that your husband didn't treat you with much respect in front of your visitors.

"Then there's Rose. She had been bossed about by Walter all her life and may have flipped when she heard that her father was changing his will. Cordelia... well, I'm not sure why Cordelia would want Walter out of the way, but she's related by marriage and there are always strange secrets in families."

Cordelia raised her eyes up to the ceiling and shook her head in frustration. "Hattie, is that all you have, strange secrets in families? All this is guesswork on your part. Please at least try to stick to the facts as you know them."

Hattie looked nonplussed. "Well, there's something fishy going on between you and George and neither of you will come clean about it which is highly suspicious. As for me, well I have no idea what my reasoning could be, but let's just say that Walter said something to upset me and I lost my temper. Feel free to check in the village with everyone who knows me to see what kind of a character I am." She put the pencil down on the table and it rolled across to the middle.

"How convenient that you are the only one without a motive," said Florence with a bitchy tone to her shrill voice. She turned round from the window and crossed her arms.

"Thank you Hattie," said Harry, ignoring Florence, and sounding weary. "That was clear enough, but I really don't know what to do next. Most of us had a motive."

"It simply must be George," spat out Florence, glaring at him. "He was the last person to see Walter alive."

"Not me," said George as everyone turned to stare at him. "The murderer was the last person to see Walter alive, and I am not he, or she. Anyway, the murder could have happened at any time yesterday. It certainly didn't happen today as he had obviously been in that water for some time. You women are not out of the picture I'm afraid."

"None of us women would dare to do such an awful thing," said Florence in solidarity of the women, trying to draw them over to her side. "Would we girls?"

No one said anything but instead continued to stare at George.

"Have you any ideas as to what we should do now?" asked Aubrey looking at Harry.

"Not really. It's early but I think we had better all go to bed," said Harry. "This has been a nasty shock and we are not getting anywhere going round in circles accusing each other. Things could turn nasty if we keep talking like this. In the morning we will have clearer heads and someone may have remembered something by then. The gardeners will come and finish removing the fallen tree so we can get help from the village. So unless anyone has anything constructive to say, let's go up."

He stood up and walked on wobbly legs to the door, opening it to let everyone out. They all trouped dutifully upstairs and disappeared into their bedrooms.

Chapter 12

Around two o'clock in the morning a scream rang out, loud and insistent, and Harry jumped out of bed and rushed to the door, throwing it open at once. Joseph, whose bedroom happened to be opposite, was standing in the corridor in his pyjamas and was joined almost immediately by George.

"It sounds as if it's coming from Cordelia's room." George leapt across the landing back the way he had appeared from and sprang at Cordelia's door. It crashed open, rebounding against the wall, and he flicked the light switch on. Cordelia had stopped screaming but was in bed sobbing loudly.

"What happened? What is it, Cordelia?" George's face filled with concern. He grabbed hold of her arms.

Harry and Joseph came through the doorway followed by the rest of the household. They had all been woken up from the depths of their reveries by her screams.

"I woke up and saw someone standing in my room. Their shadow was on the wall," she swallowed, looking suddenly very vulnerable. "I must have been the next target. I think they were going to kill me too."

Hattie gasped. "Oh no, Cordelia, surely not." She sat down on the bed next to her and handed her a handkerchief that she got out of her dressing gown pocket. "Wipe your tears away. It may well have been a bad dream and, on waking, you noticed the shadows of the trees outside creeping across the wall."

"Yes, that must have been it," said Aubrey in a gentle voice. "What possible reason could any of us have for killing you? I think we're all a little overwrought because of what has happened to Walter."

"My dear, can you give us a reason as to why someone would want to murder you?" asked Blanche quickly.

"No." Cordelia shook her head.

"You didn't see or hear anything with regards to Walter being killed?"

"Honestly, no."

"Then it must have been just your imagination getting the better of you, my dear."

"You seemed to get to your door rather quickly, Jo," said Harry suddenly.

"What do you mean?" stammered Joseph. "I opened my door at the same time as you did."

"No you didn't. You were out in the corridor already, and I thought I was pretty quick on the uptake. I was practically outside the door within seconds of waking."

"I was there at the same time I tell you," practically whimpered Joseph. "Anyway, what about George?"

"What about me?" George turned away from Cordelia and looked up at him with narrow slit-like eyes.

"You sprang across the corridor from the opposite direction to where your bedroom is," squeaked out Joseph in triumph.

Everyone turned and looked at George, suspicion once again rising up like bile in their throats.

"Well if you must know, I had been to the library to borrow a book as I couldn't sleep," replied George in disgust. "Your petty suspicions have no grounds whatsoever."

"This is not helping. If no one has anything helpful to say, I suggest we go back to bed," said Harry stifling a yawn. "Thankfully Cordelia, you are fine. Can everyone please go back to their rooms, and it may be prudent to lock your doors once you are there."

They all disappeared out of Cordelia's room and went back to their own rooms, George somewhat reluctantly, and soon the sound of keys turning in the locks was heard.

Cordelia jumped out of bed, locked her door too, and shivered as she got back in and pulled the covers right up to her nose. She didn't think she would sleep again and lay for ages watching the shadows of the trees creeping across the wall in the moonlight and listening to their branches scratching at the window.

The next morning everyone woke to the sound of axes splintering the timber of the fallen tree. The gardeners had arrived and were trying to clear a path through the driveway. It wasn't an easy task with the tree lying heavily on top of the gates. They worked diligently as, one by one the household surfaced and made their way downstairs.

George and Aubrey had skipped breakfast and were helping the men, having donned some old work clothes they had found in the hall cupboard.

Harry had been preparing to walk to the village to inform the police as the telephone was still dead, but Joseph had disagreed and stopped him as he was pulling on his walking boots.

"Look here," he said. "I trust you Harry, but maybe not everyone else here does. You can't disappear. What if you were taking Florence's jewels with you, or even the gun that shot Walter? We really should all stay together until the police get here."

Harry reluctantly agreed and went off to get one of the under-gardeners to go to the village in his place.

From then on it was a waiting game. They all sat about with weary countenances, surreptitiously eyeing each other with suspicion, awaiting the inevitable. Blanche half-heartedly occupied herself with her embroidery, but no one else could summon up the mental energy to do anything, not even talk.

Eventually they heard the sound of bells, and the roar of engines in the distance. Harry jumped to his feet and rushed out to the drive to meet the ambulance van and police inspector while the others remained where they were.

Preliminaries over, Harry led the way to the lake. The inspector followed him through the boathouse and down the spiral staircase, trying not to let his admiration show. Once they reached the end of the passage and went through the door he looked over the folly in surprise. He had heard about it before, but never given much thought to the work that must have gone into engineering the building. Doing his best not to appear too interested in it he focussed instead on the body of Walter Sinnet lying prone on the floor. The gunshot wound was noted before he turned him over to see if there were any other injuries. Lastly he put his hand into the waterlogged pockets to see if he could find anything of interest there, but they were empty.

The folly was then thoroughly looked over and Walter's body examined by the medical crew that had come in the ambulance. Photographs were taken and then at last the inspector released the body to be removed by stretcher and it was whisked away in the ambulance to the accompaniment of unnecessary sirens.

Inspector Marcus Thomas had been enjoying a leisurely breakfast with his ten-year-old son James. The storm had been severe in the village and a tree had unfortunately (or fortunately as some of the children had said) fallen through the school roof rendering it impossible to use.

Mopping up the last of his egg with some bread, he laughed at a witty comment offered by James and saw out of the corner of his eye one of Witton Park's gardeners coming up the path, holding his side and breathing in large gulps of air.

He wolfed down the remains of his breakfast and buttoned up his jacket before making his way to the door.

"Sir," panted the young lad outside. "You're needed up at the big house. There's been a murder!"

Within half an hour the ambulance had rumbled out of the village and made its way up the hill taking the exhausted gardener back up with it, and Inspector Thomas had followed, James in tow.

The inspector was a distinguished looking man in his late forties and had dark hair with a few telltale grey ones peeping through and reminding him of his age. He had worked his way up the ranks of the police force and had finally settled at the revered role of detective inspector. He loved his job and had a sharp brain used to getting results and was well respected in the village. It irked him that none of his cases involved much brainwork and he wondered how he would fare if he were ever to get a complex case to solve.

"Now my son," he said as the car negotiated the steep incline of the hill in front. "I want you to remain in the car; you can't come in the house with me. This is a murder investigation and children can have no part to play in it. You can sit on the back seat and reflect on your lessons. You may not have school but this is not a play day."

"But Father," protested James. "I can use my brains by helping you solve the crime!"

"You're not allowed, my boy. Now heed what I say and wait for me here."

He parked the car next to the ambulance just outside where the driveway gates had been; noting the huge tree that had been hacked at to make a passageway through. It certainly was a big one. The gardeners were milling about, trying to tidy up branches and piles of leaves and get them ready to throw on the bonfire.

"Yes Father." James twirled his hat around his fingers and assumed an air of self-pity.

Inspector Thomas laughed and patted the boy on the back. He alighted from the vehicle and found Harry coming towards him from the house.

Chapter 13

Sitting in the library where Harry had dispatched him after viewing the body, Inspector Thomas looked through Hattie's notes in a thoughtful manner. He had questioned Harry while he was there and Harry had also given him some information as to who the guests were. He sat back, stretched his legs out under the vast leather topped oak desk, and pondered. Harry had told him to ring the bell for the butler when he wanted anything, but first he wanted to have a look around the house.

He stood up and pushed the chair back, moving swiftly to the door. Opening it he wandered into the hallway, which was large and had quite a few doors going off from it with a grand curved staircase winding up to the first floor. The doors revealed a huge morning room, breakfast room, dining room, formal lounge, kitchen, scullery, and butler's pantry. There was a telephone room, which was more of a booth than a room, a study, which also housed an extension telephone, and a rather large ballroom, which looked as if it had only been used for storage, as it was full of packing cases and wooden boxes. A large conservatory had been built at the side of the ballroom and was chock-full of palm trees and tropical looking plants with big red spiky flowers on them that the inspector hadn't encountered before. These were presumably sent back when Mr Sinnet came back from working in America. It looked as if there had been some storm damage in there as some of the plants were strewn across the floor amongst dirt and broken glass from one of the windows. The last room was the drawing room where he could hear voices coming from behind the door. He didn't open that door.

A tall and imposing grandfather clock stood against the wall looking haughtily down at him and an ornate hat-stand stood bare next to it. It was obvious that it was more of a decorative statement than a practical object. An old-fashioned chunky mahogany cupboard with drawers nestled self-consciously under the stairwell, looking conspicuous against the feminine touches that rather forcedly surrounded it. A bowl of violets sat on top looking uncomfortable, reminding the inspector wryly of a large man wearing a lady's hat. The walls going up the stairs were decorated in red silk and had oil paintings of horses and dogs hung on them. There were no ancestors there, presumably because this family hadn't come from nobility. Mr Sinnet had made his own money as was well documented. The inspector half expected to see a large oil painting of Walter himself glowering down from one of the walls, but there wasn't one.

Marble plinths were dotted about with large potted plants on some of them, and a miniature copy of the famous statue of David stood on the corner of the stairwell where it wound sharply upwards. Inspector Thomas touched it as he walked past and it felt cold and hard.

Upstairs, there were more paintings and a beautiful chandelier that would be the envy of most people. At the end of the corridor, which had rather a lot of bedrooms leading off from it, a suit of armour stood in front of a large window that looked out over the lake. Everything reeked of wealth but not in a classy way. Money seemed to ooze out of every pore, but it didn't matter if anything clashed, as long as it looked expensive, or so it seemed to him. Maybe it was just sour grapes pondered the inspector thinking of his own little, sparsely furnished cottage back down in the village.

He went back downstairs noting that his home would fit into the hallway comfortably with room to spare and went to the library and sat down. Etiquette told him that he should see the lady of the house first, so he reached out his hand and rang the bell, subconsciously wishing he had one at home.

When Blanche entered the room, Inspector Thomas could see at once that she had been crying. Her eyes were red and puffy, and her hands were shaking slightly.

"Mrs Sinnet?" The inspector stood up with a straight back until she had sat down, then he sat down himself. "My name is Inspector Thomas and I am here to find out what has happened to your husband. I'm sorry to be intrusive in your time of grief but please, if you would, give me your version of events this weekend. Leave nothing out, however insignificant it may seem to you."

Blanche looked up at the inspector, took a deep breath, and began to talk. She told him how her niece Cordelia had recently become a widow and had travelled over from America to stay with them to get over the shock of it. She had been with them nearly a week. Regarding the weekend house party, her childhood friend, Aubrey Sapping, had been the first to arrive. She had asked him herself. She had also asked a girl called Hattie Abberton, who lived in the village, and had made herself almost indispensable at the women's group. She thought she would be good company for Cordelia. Joseph Brewer and his wife Florence had been invited to stay by her husband Walter. Walter's oldest friend was Joseph's father, but he was away and so had not been asked. Also asked by Walter was a man called George Brown who was American and had been keen to do business with Sinnet Industries. Apart from them, there were her two children Harry and Rose.

She continued to talk, allowing herself the memory of their dinner together on the first evening.

"We all went to view the folly afterwards," she recollected. "Walter was ever so excited showing it off and I could tell he loved everyone's admiration of it. The following day was passed in recreational pursuits, although Walter had been working in the morning, and that night the storm had come in full force. Walter did not come to dinner or even back to the house at all."

"Thank you Mrs Sinnet," smiled the inspector as Blanche's hurried words came to a faltering end. "Was he the only person not to turn up for dinner?"

"Well no. Joseph and Florence Brewer stayed away and so did George Brown."

"I see," said Inspector Thomas, hastily writing down on his pad. "Did your niece and Mr Brown travel here on the same boat from America?"

"Well I never even thought to ask that. I would have said no, but earlier she admitted to having known him before this weekend. I guess she meant she had met him on the boat. George told us he was in England a few days on other business before making his way here."

"Thank you. Now, can you tell me if anyone had a grudge against your husband?"

Blanche looked up, startled. "Well, no, not really. Of course, one does pick up enemies in business but no one wanted him dead to my knowledge."

"He recently returned from working in America. Did he come back in any kind of hurry?" asked Inspector Thomas carefully.

"Well, not in a hurry exactly, but we weren't really expecting it to be so soon, now that you ask. I was surprised to see him when he turned up, as I'd been half expecting him to write to us to make us all up sticks and emigrate to be with him out there."

"Would you have been willing to do that?"

"Well, I didn't really want to. I've only ever known England, but he was my husband and if he'd wanted it, I would have had no choice. I'm not so sure about the children though. They're too settled here to my mind. Anyway, Walter came home and threw himself into improving the property here, and had been doing so from abroad too, so I suppose he wanted to remain here in the long run. I take it you've seen the folly under the lake?"

"Yes, it's magnificent," said the inspector generously. "Can I ask why the ballroom is not used? I noticed it was full of packing cases."

Blanche looked up. "Well I'm afraid Walter did not like dancing, or anything he deemed frivolous. His plan was to turn the ballroom into something quite different. He wanted to design something spectacular in there to impress clients and prospective clients. It was something he was working on."

"So nobody threatened him with his life then?"

"No! There was unrest, for a while, from the farmers that had their land taken back from them. Walter no longer wanted to rent the fields out as he had plans for making the lake, but I don't believe anyone would kill him because of it. Everything blew over almost as soon as it had begun."

"Unlike the storm," murmured the inspector. "Do you have a list of those farmers so I can contact them?"

"I'm not sure I do. At least, I've never seen a list. You are welcome to look through his files if you think you might find something to help you. Alternatively, Mr Marlin the solicitor will have them, as he had drawn up the original contracts so I'll let you have his details."

"Thank you. Was Mr Marlin on good terms with your husband?"

"Oh yes. Mr Marlin dealt with all of Walter's legal business and was paid more than handsomely too. He had nothing to complain of to my knowledge." Blanche looked faintly reproving.

"He was meant to be here this weekend but cancelled at the last minute," said the inspector echoing what Harry had told him earlier.

"It was the weather. It put him off and I can't say I blame him as I've never encountered a more brutal storm."

"I see from these notes that Mr Sapping was heard saying he would like to kill your husband to set you free from him." Inspector Thomas glanced down at the notebook. "Is Mr Sapping in love with you?"

"Aubrey? Of course not! He was not serious; it was merely an innocuous remark that's all. He is a friend and simply wouldn't do anything to hurt me. In fact, he wouldn't hurt anyone and he knew I was loyal to my husband."

Inspector Thomas avoided looking directly at her. "So who do you think could have shot him then, Mrs Sinnet?"

"I'm afraid I couldn't say, but I can't imagine that it was any of us. It must have been a mad man loose on the estate."

"Humour me if you please, Mrs Sinnet. What if you had to point the finger at someone here?"

"If it was imperative to pick on someone here, although I'm not happy to do so, I suppose the most likely person would be George. None of us knew him, although…"

"Yes?"

"Nothing. I meant nothing. My husband had been in contact with him but none of us had met him before this weekend."

"Apart from your niece."

"That's just speculation at the moment."

"And what is your limited opinion on George Brown's character?"

"Well, he seems very nice. A bit reserved and not particularly happy to talk about himself but he doesn't seem suspicious at all."

"How was your relationship with your husband, Mrs Sinnet? Were you happy?"

"Inspector, I find that question impertinent. We were perfectly content. My husband was a little difficult as I am sure you will hear from other people, but he did not deserve to be shot because of it. He was suffering with his health and refused to seek medical help. I had a feeling he was dying so if you are suggesting I killed him, therein lies the proof that I had no need to do such a thing. It would have happened naturally pretty soon of its own accord."

"He was a sick man? Was anyone else aware about the condition of his health, Mrs Sinnet? Anyone that could corroborate your story?"

"I'm afraid not. His health issues were kept between Walter and myself, although you could ask the doctor who originally guessed that he had consumption if you want to find out if I'm telling the truth or not." Blanche held the inspector's gaze levelly. "I will find his details for you. I'm sure I still have them somewhere."

"I'm not suggesting you are not telling the truth, Mrs Sinnet. I am merely trying to get to the bottom of all of this, as it is my job to find out who murdered your husband. Please do get me the details of the doctor as soon as you can, though, along with Mr Marlin's."

"I will go and find them for you at once."

"Before you go, please can you tell me who benefits from your husband's will?"

Blanche, who had been making her way to the door, stopped and turned slowly around. "Harry inherits the estate and I get everything else, as it currently stands. Rose gets to live in the house for as long as she wishes and inherits my share of the inheritance on my demise."

"Are you certain of that?"

"Yes. Well, no not absolutely certain. That is what I understood from my husband."

"How was your husband hoping to alter his will this week?"

77

"I don't know Inspector. He probably wasn't going to change anything. It was one of his frequent threats to upset the children but I usually just ignored it."

"So you didn't show any interest in the fact that he was potentially going to make a life-changing decision involving yourself and your children?"

"Life-changing? No Inspector, I did not pay any attention to it. As I said, it was a frequent threat of his and Walter would not have left us destitute whatever anyone may say about him. Mr Marlin will be able to tell you exactly what was in the will when you talk to him."

After a few more questions the inspector could see that Blanche did not want to say anything more and decided to let her go.

"Thank you Mrs Sinnet. That will do for now. Please could you ask your niece to come in and see me next?"

Shortly afterwards, Cordelia came in through the door and sat down, looking suspicious and on edge.

"Mrs... I'm sorry; I only have your first name."

"Mrs, er, Mrs Brown. You can call me Cordelia."

"What a coincidence, Mrs Brown. There is also a Mr Brown staying here."

"Yes," muttered Cordelia. "A common name as I'm sure you must know."

"I hear you are a widow, Mrs Brown."

"That is so, Inspector, but you are surely not here to question me about my marital status?"

"That is quite correct," said Inspector Thomas with a shrewd look in his eye. "Would you like to tell me anything about the Mr Brown that is here this weekend?"

"What could I possibly tell you about him, Inspector?" Cordelia's set smile did not quite reach her eyes. "You would be better off asking him yourself."

"I have a vague idea of what you could tell me, Mrs Brown. I must inform you that anything said that is not relevant to the investigation will not be shared with the rest of the household or indeed anyone else."

Cordelia swallowed and looked down at the desk, not seeming quite able to meet the inspector's sharp eyes. A silence hung heavily between them for a few seconds.

"Did you travel to England on the same boat as George Brown?" Inspector Thomas continued with his questioning.

"I really couldn't say; I'm afraid."

"Please let me see your travel papers as soon as you can, Mrs Brown."

To try to put her at ease the inspector asked her some questions about the rest of the household to which she replied curtly.

Glancing out of the window, Inspector Thomas noticed James laughing with one of the under-gardeners and bouncing up and down on one of the overturned gate leaves. He smiled to himself. James wasn't in the car, but at least he was keeping out of mischief. He tapped his pen on the notepad and brought his attention back to Cordelia.

"Mrs Brown, can you give me a picture of who Walter Sinnet was?"

"He was my aunt's husband; an entrepreneur of massive proportions. She married him when he started out as an assayer and had little money and he then went on to make a fortune speculating on mines."

"Did you like him?"

Cordelia looked at him scornfully. "I don't see what that has got to do with anything, but seeing as you ask, no I didn't like him. He was not trustworthy and seemed only to care about himself and amassing as much wealth as possible. I don't think he cared about people."

"Not even his family?"

"Not even them."

"I see. What did his family think about him?"

"You'd have to ask them that question as I can't answer for them. I have nothing further to say at present, Inspector." She rose tentatively as if she was expecting to be stopped at any second and left the room.

Chapter 14

Inspector Thomas sat back in his chair, glanced up at the deer head that was mounted on the wall, and contemplated on what he had heard so far. His thoughts then turned to practicalities. He would have to get a team up here and get the house and grounds searched. The jewellery and the weapon had to be around somewhere. No one had had the chance to leave Witton Park as of yet. The local farmers would have to be questioned and the doctor and Mr Marlin located. Mr Marlin may well have cancelled coming for the weekend, but could he possibly have come anyway and fired that shot? Did he have a reason to do so? Also, the list of passengers on the American liner would have to be checked. He rang for the butler to see if the telephone was back up and running and was told within a few minutes that it was. He gave him instructions to get word to police headquarters as soon as possible.

Joseph came in next. He sashayed through the door with his monocle firmly in place and sat down.

"Ah, Mr Brewer," said Inspector Thomas shaking his hand. "Perhaps you could tell me a little of the events that took place this weekend?"

"Certainly Inspector." Joseph sat forward in his chair and looked thoughtful. He cast his mind back and began. "Florence, my wife, insisted we come this weekend. I wasn't very keen I have to say as the Sinnets are really my parents' friends, not ours."

"So why was she so insistent?" The inspector smiled encouragingly.

"Well, the old girl had the idea that I should talk to Walter about investing in his company. He had hinted about it in the past and had been quite insistent that it would benefit us financially."

"Do you need, er, help in that area?" asked Inspector Thomas delicately.

Joseph looked up. "Well, yes, I'm afraid so, we have nothing, but it's no secret. Well, we had Florence's jewellery, but that happened to be stolen this weekend. I really have the morbs if truth be known."

"Do you have any idea as to who the thief could be?"

"Some scoundrel, I should imagine. I'm not sure who the thief is but I feel I can't really trust anyone around here. The place needs to be searched, and those jewels returned to my wife as soon as possible."

"Would you happen to be privy to any information about Mr Sinnet's will?"

"I always thought that a will was a dead giveaway!" joshed Joseph with a snort.

"This is a murder investigation Mr Brewer, in case you had forgotten."

"Yes Inspector, I apologise. My wife always tells me that I have an inappropriate humour. I didn't have any knowledge regarding the will by the way."

"What did you think of Mr Sinnet?"

"Not much, to be honest. As I said, he was my father's friend from childhood. They were complete polar opposites though. My father is gentle and kind and generous and Walter, although generous, seemed only to be so in order to show off his tremendous wealth. Greedy and mean are the words I'd use to describe him, but that's just between ourselves."

"Was he mean to your father?"

"It's funny you should ask that question. I went to talk to Walter about investing and he told me in no uncertain terms that there was no investment to be had. It had been his idea in the first place and so I was completely flummoxed. When I was pondering it, I recalled something at the back of my mind that I still can't quite get into focus. It was something to do with him letting my father down, but I'm unaware of the details. I have a feeling that Father lost money, though."

"I'd like to have a word with your father. Please pass his contact details to me when you get a chance."

Some time later, Joseph left the library and went to fetch Florence.

"Well, I can't think what I can tell him," she said to Joseph as she hurried across the hall patting her hair in place. "I can't tell him anything."

Secretly she was looking forward to airing her views on everyone there. She stopped outside the library door, applied some lipstick, and then entered, shutting the door determinedly behind her.

"I'm here, Inspector. Florence Brewer's the name. How can I be of help?"

Inspector Thomas was momentarily nonplussed. He looked down at his notes and then began to speak.

"What can you tell me about your weekend so far, Mrs Brewer?" he said. "Please start at the beginning and don't leave anything out. I'd like the events in sequence and your opinions on each of the people here."

Florence took a deep breath and started on the semi-rehearsed speech that had been going round her head. After what seemed an interminable amount of time, she ground to a halt.

Inspector Thomas felt a bit dizzy when she'd stopped talking and shook his head. All he could see was the lipstick on her front teeth as she chattered away incessantly, and all he could smell was the waft of her over-sweet perfume. He got up and opened the window.

Now that Florence had got all of that out, the inspector felt he could start to ask her some sensible questions to which she would no doubt now answer properly, having got everything else off her chest first.

When the Inspector Thomas had finished with Florence, he summoned Rose.

"Miss Sinnet?" He rose from his chair and motioned for her to sit down.

"Yes, I'm Miss Sinnet. Please call me Rose."

"I'm sorry for the loss of your father. However, I must ask you a few questions to try to get to the bottom of everything that has been going on here."

"That's okay, Inspector, I don't mind. I'm afraid it was no secret around here that my father and I were not exactly on the best of terms. I'm telling you before everyone else gets in there first."

"Could you tell me the reason for that?"

"He was a tyrant," burst out Rose. "He was bossy and seemed to resent me for being a girl. I think he must have been a misogynist. Mind you, Harry is a boy, and he wasn't exactly enamoured with him either. Nothing seemed to make him happy apart from making money and showing it off. I'm afraid that in essence my father was a bully, a bully in business and a bully at home."

"Can you unpack that statement a bit more?" asked the inspector carefully, writing on his pad.

"Just exactly that, Inspector, he bullied us. He ordered me around all the time and was constantly complaining. Poor Harry hid away in this room most of the time, reading. Father hated it and once threatened to burn the books, much to Harry's horror. Mother had to stop him. Nothing was right for him and we were so glad when he went away to work in America and life was peaceful and quiet."

"Did he treat your mother in the same way?"

"Not really, but Mother was so amenable when it came to him. She didn't like rocking the boat; she had her own life, her own things to take up her time. Mother organised everything here in the house, she did good works in the village, and she loved embroidery. Father more or less left her alone to get on with it."

"How did he bully in business?" Inspector Thomas leaned forward slightly, listening intently.

"Let's just say he wasn't exactly honest in his dealings, Inspector. If he could con anyone, he would do it without guilt. How do you think we got to be quite so rich?"

"Miss Sinnet, I mean Rose, who do you think shot your father?"

"I'm not sure and to be honest, I don't really care. What's done is done."

"I would appreciate all the help you can give me. You must have some idea, even if it isn't substantiated. Everything's supposition until we can prove it."

"I suspect it was the same person who took the jewels," replied Rose carefully.

"Well who do you think took the jewels?"

"I would put money on it being George Brown." Rose crossed her arms across her chest and looked defiant.

The inspector raised his eyebrows. "And what possible reason could he have for theft and murder?"

"We don't know him for starters, he could be anybody. Florence seems to think her jewellery was worth a lot of money and Joseph's father had recommended her buying it as an investment for their future..."

"Joseph's father was your father's friend, was he not?" interrupted Inspector Thomas.

"Well, yes, that's true." Rose considered the fact as if she hadn't thought about it before. "Anyway, Joseph's father is a good and honest man in my opinion and he found the jewels for her as a backup in case she needed it. George Brown claimed to be a jewel expert but when he viewed Florence's sparklers he said they were worthless. All of them! That night the jewels disappeared from under her nose. The same night, Father was murdered. My father was also a con man, Inspector and my guess is that George was conned by him. They say revenge is sweet."

"Did Mr Brown value anyone else's jewels while he was at it?"

"No I don't think so. He was reluctant to look at Florence's, which is another black mark against him. Makes one think he didn't know what he was talking about. During dinner on the first evening I showed him my ruby ring."

She held up her hand and showed the inspector the red sparkling jewel.

"What did he say about it?"

"He said it was worth a lot of money. Beginner's luck or an educated guess?"

"That remains to be seen. Tell me, what was in your father's will?"

"Will? Well, who knows? He was always changing his mind, or at least threatening to do so. As far as I know, Harry was to inherit the estate and Mother everything else."

"Everything else?"

"Yes, you know… all his assets, his company, his investments, his other properties."

"Did you not feature in this will?"

"Me? No, I don't think so," laughed Rose in amusement. "I inherit after Mother dies."

A gong sounded from the hall and Rose stood up. "That'll be luncheon. I heard your son is here. You and he would be most welcome to eat in the kitchen with the staff if you would like to."

She went out of the room leaving him looking thoughtful.

Chapter 15

That afternoon the household got restless. George was summoned to the library and went gratefully; glad to get away from the others. He shook hands with the inspector and sat down.

"How can I help you, Inspector?"

"I'd like your version of events this weekend please, Mr Brown." Inspector Thomas looked at George's shrewd eyes and waited for him to speak.

"Well, I arrived in time for pre-dinner drinks. I knew nobody here and had come to do some business with Walter Sinnet who I had been in touch with in America. This weekend was the first time we had actually met face to face."

"Did you come across by liner?"

"Yes," replied George with a puzzled face. "Why do you ask?"

"I was just wondering if you had met with Mrs Cordelia Brown on the ship. You were both travelling across from America, so it stands to reason you would have bumped into each other at some point."

"Who says we were on the same ship, Inspector?" George shifted uncomfortably in his seat.

"Purely a hunch. Now tell me what the nature of your business with Walter Sinnet was, Mr Brown." The inspector, noticing George's discomfort, decided to continue down a different path.

"Well, it was just business, Inspector. I needn't go into detail surely?"

"You are in the jewellery and precious stone business. What did that industry have to do with oil speculators like Sinnet Industries? I'm just curious so please humour me."

"Well if you must know, Walter and I had done business together before actually meeting. He would buy jewels from me and, I suppose, sell them on, or give them as gifts. It was his personal business, nothing to do with Sinnet Industries."

"Expensive jewels?"

"Well yes, very expensive."

"Do you only deal in the pricey ones?"

"No, I also sell paste jewels as I have to cater for all markets, although my main business is with the pure stones." George began to look more relaxed as he talked.

"Did Mr Sinnet ever buy the lesser expensive paste jewels?" asked Inspector Thomas, a little light going on in his head.

"Well, yes he did seeing as you ask. There had been more than one occasion when he wanted substandard jewels." He looked across the desk at the inspector who looked back with owl-like eyes, holding his gaze for several seconds.

"I see," he said eventually. "What do you mean by substandard exactly? Is that what you call the paste?"

"Well, I mean fakes, Inspector. Common or garden paste jewels but made to look real. Paste is not illegal, but I believe he was selling them on as the real deal."

"Do you know what happened to the pastes he purloined from you?"

"I certainly know what happened to some of them. They made their way to Florence Brewer's house. She asked me to value her jewellery over the weekend and I recognised them at once. I told her they were worthless, but she didn't believe me. Her father-in-law had recommended them to her to secure her future. He hadn't seen them himself, I believe, but had been told by Walter Sinnet that they were worth a lot of money and that he had got them for a good price."

"Mr Brewer's father was Walter Sinnet's friend was he not?"

"So I understand. Some friend!"

"I'd like to ask you about Rose Sinnet's ruby ring?"

"What about it? Has it gone missing?"

"No, but I hear you told her it was an expensive item."

"That's true, I did."

"Would it interest you to know that it is a piece of cheap costume jewellery?"

For a moment George looked confused, then he laughed heartily. "Nice try Inspector, I see you're testing me. That ring is a very expensive pigeon blood ruby. I can tell that by the colour and clarity of the jewel, but don't take my word for it. Get a second opinion if you like."

"Mr Brown, you say you arrived in time for pre-dinner drinks and that you didn't know anybody here?" said the inspector, going back to the previous subject. "How is it that you were spotted talking to Mrs Cordelia Brown in the grounds beforehand?"

"Nothing suspicious there I'm afraid, Inspector," retorted George. "We happened to be both strolling around the grounds at the same time and ran into each other."

"Are you a married man, Mr Brown?"

"I can't see what that has to do with anything?" George's eyes narrowed and he swallowed hard.

"Please just humour me, Mr Brown, and answer the question."

"I am not married."

"If I take a look into your life in America, which will be long and laborious, but necessary, will I find anything contrary to that which you are telling me now?"

George sighed and got a handkerchief out of his pocket, mopping his forehead with it. He was silent for a few seconds.

"Right, look here, Inspector. All I can tell you is that I did not murder Walter. You have to take my word for that."

"I'm afraid that is something I simply cannot do, Mr Brown. To save yourself from the threat of being arrested for something you did not do, you need to be one hundred percent honest with me, there is no other way. If you would like to have a think and come back to see me later that is fine."

George got up and half stumbled to the door, disappearing out of it quickly.

Aubrey was summoned next and sauntered in, a grin on his face. "Inspector, I'm Aubrey Sapping. How can I help?" They shook hands and Aubrey sat down and waited to be questioned.

"So, Mr Sapping, I hear you are a good friend of Blanche Sinnet?"

"That is so, Inspector. We have known each other since we were small children and have kept in touch over the years."

"Were you also friends with Mr Walter Sinnet?" The question was asked in a gentle voice.

Aubrey looked up. "No, Inspector, I couldn't stand the man, I may as well tell you that from the start. He was not a pleasant character and only seemed to care about money and showing off. His wife and kids were second best to everything and we disliked each other immensely."

"And yet it didn't bother you to accept his hospitality. I take it you were, or are, in love with Mrs Sinnet? I hope you don't object to my question."

Aubrey laughed ruefully. "No, no objection here, old chap. Yes, I love her, always have, and always will, but she only ever had eyes for her husband. A good and faithful woman she is. However, if your questions are leading to the inevitable, I should tell you now that I did not kill Walter for reasons of jealousy and wanting Blanche for myself. No sir. I left the folly before the other men and was back in the drawing room with Blanche within minutes. I had dinner with her, Rose, Harry, and Hattie after that and then went up to my bedroom."

"Did you stay in your bedroom all night?"

"No. In the middle of the night the wind blew the front door open, and I rushed down to help Harry, who happened to be there. George Brown appeared at the top of the stairs and came to help too. There was no way anyone could have left the house during the night. They would have been blown clean away."

"Who do you think killed him, Mr Sapping?"

"I really have no idea, but I'd like to shake him by the hand. I can see by your face that you think me callous, but you didn't know him. Anyway, my guess would be some poor mutt that was conned out of a small fortune. I've heard there was discontent overseas and also as near as the village. There are always enemies when you tread on people to get to the top."

"Did he tread on people then?"

"Most definitely. Did you know he was known as Midas behind his back because everything he touched seemed to turn to gold? That didn't help him in the end though, did it?"

After a few more questions, Aubrey left the room and was replaced by a nervous looking Hattie.

"Ah, Miss Abberton," said Inspector Thomas. "I believe I have seen you before in the village but never made your acquaintance."

"Hello Inspector," replied Hattie with a shaky smile. "Yes, I live in the village with my mother."

"Please tell me what you can about the weekend so far and how you came to be here."

Hattie began to talk, starting with her surprising and unexpected invitation from Blanche.

"Mrs Sinnet has been somewhat of an inspiration to me what with her good works and selfless giving in the village for the women who are less fortunate than her. I've always tried to help those that are less fortunate than me but Mrs Sinnet is a marvel and I have enjoyed getting to know her a bit. I'm not quite sure why she asked me in particular, but she said it was because her niece had been recently bereaved and she thought we could be friends."

"Have you become friends?"

"No, not really. Cordelia is quite prickly and not always easy to have a comfortable conversation with I'm afraid." Hattie looked slightly guilty as if she were talking badly of a friend.

"I'm sure you have heard the village gossip about the discontent there at what Walter Sinnet was doing to the landscape of the area?"

"Yes, and I was prepared to hate the place but in actual fact I love it. He may have got rid of arable land, but he has put carp in the lake and all manner of other beautiful fish. Plenty of wildlife will come to the area and live in the forests he's planted, and I for one think that's great."

"So you like the place?"

"Well it is rather ostentatious, but yes I'd say that I do like it."

"Do you think someone from the village could have plotted to get rid of Walter?"

"Possibly, but I don't know anyone to have made any threats. Any would-be murderer would have had to have been very lucky to have managed to catch Mr Sinnet on his own like that. Anyway, how they would have negotiated the walls or gate I don't know. I suppose they must have got in and out again before the storm damage."

After a few minutes Inspector Thomas dismissed Hattie and began to peruse his notes.

Chapter 16

James was enjoying his day off school and decided to assist his father in finding the murderer. He babbled away to the gardeners talking nineteen to the dozen, trying to get information out of them, but they hardly knew a thing. They were all speculating as they worked, gossiping away, and sharing any information they had on the guests staying there, which was not much. They worked hard, shovelling the debris up from the storm and soon the bonfire was lit, and began to pop and crackle merrily away. The wood was damp, which caused a lot of smoke that stung their eyes and then rose high into the air, sending out little sparks. The gardeners poked and prodded at it, enjoying the heat, and presently James slipped away unnoticed.

He pushed past the rhododendrons, getting his shoulder and arm wet, and felt irritated with the branches hanging across the pathway. Someone really should cut them back. Reaching the edge of the lake, he looked out across to the statue and wondered what the folly looked like beneath it. He'd heard about it, who hadn't? It had been the talk of the village for months seeing as most of the manual labourers there had been involved in its construction. Hadn't one of them died building it? He couldn't quite remember the details.

James skirted the edge of the lake, grinning and waving at the ducks gliding across the top, making his way towards the boathouse. That must surely house the entrance to the folly. Quietly opening the door, he pretended he was an inspector, stalking his prey. He tiptoed across to the door behind the rubber plant and marvelled at the spiral staircase leading downwards. Still on the tips of his toes James made his way down to the tunnel below and ran his hands along the walls as he walked down the passageway towards the folly. He was a policeman, strong and clever, tracking the criminal with stealth. He was vaguely wondering to himself why the lights were on when he heard a noise beyond the door at the end. The hairs on the back of his neck rose, and he stopped dead in his tracks. Who was there? The murderer must be back, covering up his tracks. He let out a little yelp of fright and turned to sprint back up the corridor, when he heard the door squeak slowly open on hinges that already needed oiling despite being new.

"Stop right there," roared a voice, and James froze. He turned and looked round as if in slow motion and flattened himself against the wall cringing in terror.

A figure stood framed against the doorway, his dark shadow lengthening as he moved and looking chillingly distorted.

"What are you doing here?" The voice echoed up towards him as the figure came out of the room.

James almost fainted with relief when he saw the uniformed constable coming towards him and managed to find his voice. "Sir, I'm here with my father, Sir. That's Inspector Thomas, Sir. I was exploring. I wanted to see the folly." His voice came in quick bursts.

"Right," the voice softened slightly. "Well you shouldn't be here but seeing as we have finished fingerprinting the gun cabinet now, I'll let you have a little peak at the room. Come on, quick sharp, mind."

James trotted towards him and inched past him into the folly. He nodded in an official manner at the other police officers as he had often seen his father do in the past. They were putting their equipment away and looked serious. He stood open-mouthed, staring up at the glass roof in wonder. He turned around taking it all in, savouring it all to share with the boys at school. They would be so jealous that he had been the one to see it. Everyone he had spoken to at school had an opinion on what it would look like, but it was far more spectacular than even James had imagined. It somehow didn't seem real. He made up his mind to be an architect or engineer when he was older and thought about the projects he would bring into being. When famous in his field he would smile and fondly remember this moment; the moment he had known what his destiny would be.

The police constable that had let him in was wandering about the room with his hands behind his back looking important. James sauntered over to him. "So what do you think of the folly, Constable?" he asked in his most grown up voice.

Constable Turner grinned at him. "Very impressive isn't it? Wish I could show it to my wife!"

"I was just thinking how jealous my school friends would be."

One of the fingerprint officers looked over at them and Constable Turner cleared his throat and stood up a bit straighter.

"That's it now, son, you'd better hop it. We need to lock up and go to the main house." His gruff voice brought James sharply back to reality.

He said thank you politely and left the folly, skipping up the corridor back to the boathouse. His beating heart was still racing after his earlier fright and he wanted to get back to the gardeners and see how the fire was doing. The branches of the rhododendrons reached out their fingers and grabbed hold of him as he navigated his way round them, shaking water all over him and making him wet again.

"Right, that's it." James was angry now. "This bush has gone too far this time."

He reached out and snapped one of the branches with his hands. He pushed it back and wedged it behind the main trunk with difficulty and then did the same with a larger and longer branch. It was enjoyable. Being a police inspector was no longer an option, nor even an engineer or architect, he was now a gardener in the grounds of the grand house. He had a team of under-gardeners all accountable to him and ready to do his bidding.

"Silly overgrown plant," he said out loud, kicking out at the dense foliage. He kicked out again and his foot dislodged something from a lower branch, which made a thud as it hit the ground. What on earth was that? Scrabbling about on his knees, James reached out to see what it was. He felt around, curiosity getting the better of him, and his fingertips touched something hard, cold, and metal. He strained to reach it but the thing, whatever it was, got wedged against a root that was jutting out of the ground. Snapping one of the branches off the main body of the bush, James poked it towards the root trying to free the thing. It was tricky, but he felt compelled to find out what was hiding in there. He managed to free it at last and gave himself an imaginary pat on the back, dragging the item across the ground towards himself with the stick.

An excitement rose up in him as he realised what it was. A gun! It must surely be the murder weapon. He had to get it to his father at once, as there would be fingerprints all over it. As he began to get to his feet he sensed someone behind him and stuffed the gun into his pocket quick as a flash.

Before he could turn, there was a wallop and something hit him on the back of the head. He stumbled forward and felt hands pushing him deep into the rhododendrons. That was when everything went black.

Chapter 17

Inspector Thomas had left the library and was wandering around the house. The other policemen had come in and were searching the rooms so he joined them. Harry came along too in his new role as man of the house and sauntered along, hands behind his back.

"So did you learn anything interesting this morning Sir?" asked Harry in a polite voice.

Inspector Thomas gave him a sideways glance. "Yes, Mr Sinnet, I always learn interesting titbits of information from people. The human psyche is a fascinating subject."

"Have you got a suspect in mind for the murder of my father?"

"Everyone here is a suspect I'm afraid, Sir... even your good self."

"Well yes, I guess that's true. I don't suppose it's any good my telling you I didn't do it?"

"Not really, Sir, no." Inspector Thomas smiled wryly.

"Inspector, I've just remembered something that could be important. I overheard my father shouting at someone on the telephone in the morning before he was killed."

"Is that so? Do you have any idea who he was shouting at and for what reason?"

"I can't even begin to guess and only just recalled it this second. He was shouting that he did not react well to threats. At the time I guessed it was one of the American investors who was let down by him, but I can't say for sure."

"I see. I wish you had remembered that earlier. Are any of the investors in this country at the moment?"

"I honestly couldn't say, but even if they were, there was no way on or off the property in that storm."

"Do you think anyone from the village could have been the caller, one of the farmers perhaps?"

"Well, of course, anything is possible, Inspector, but I thought all that unrest had died down. They had all been paid compensation."

"I need to get that call traced as soon as possible."

Suddenly a shout came from one of the rooms and a policeman rushed out onto the landing. "The jewels, Sir… we've found them."

He held out a linen pillowcase that had a fair amount of necklaces, rings, and bracelets inside it.

"Whose room is this?" Inspector Thomas quickly reached out and took the pillowcase from him.

"Why it's George Brown's room," said Harry. "Rose was right… of all the thieving cads!"

Florence upended the pillowcase onto the table in the drawing room and scrabbled about, counting everything. The household had been summoned there by the inspector, and all sat or stood around the room watching her.

She finally gave a sigh of relief. "I can't believe it. Everything is here. I've never been so grateful in all my life." She smiled a watery smile at Joseph who smiled back, looking tense. "Where did you find it?"

"It was found in Mr Brown's room," said Inspector Thomas looking directly at George who immediately turned pale.

"What?" It was almost a whisper. "But it couldn't have been in my room, I didn't take the jewels. Where in my room?"

"The pillowcase was found pushed under your wardrobe, right at the back." Inspector Thomas' voice hardened. "Perhaps you'd like to tell us how it got there?"

"I tell you I don't know anything about it," said poor George, really looking quite ill. "If I'd stolen them I most definitely wouldn't have hidden them in my own room!" He looked over at Cordelia who was looking petrified.

"Double bluff," squeaked Joseph.

A hard expression crossed Rose's face. "I had a feeling it was you. A bit obvious, you telling Florence her jewels were worthless, and then them disappearing all of a sudden like that."

"But they were, I mean are, worthless," spluttered George. "The Brewers were conned."

"Conned?" exploded Florence in anger. "Joseph's father would not do that to us."

"Maybe not your father-in-law," replied George. "He could have been conned from another source, though. Think about it, who got him those jewels?"

"Well, they came from Walter," said Florence beginning to look a bit worried.

Rose sat down suddenly. "Oh no," she whispered looking to Harry for support.

Harry was standing by the fireplace with his back to the room. He turned slowly around, and looked at his sister.

"Well, I think we all know that our father wasn't exactly an honourable man but do you really suppose he would dupe his friend on purpose?"

Joseph, stammering, piped up, "I recall him upsetting Father on one occasion. He wanted Father to invest money into one of his schemes and I'm pretty sure Father ended up losing a lot of dough though I can't remember any details clearly. Now I come to think about it that could be why he works so hard. He has to make back his loss so he can retire and enjoy his life." Joseph's monocle fell out, and he let it swing on its chain, watching it rotate slowly around.

"He wouldn't," said Blanche in anguish. "Deceive his oldest friend? I can't believe it." She crossed her arms. "If this is true I will make sure you are paid back every penny."

She crossed the room and patted Florence on her shoulder and Florence looked up at her gratefully.

"Anyway, I am still wondering why you were on the wrong part of the landing the night Cordelia had an intruder," said Joseph to George. "Maybe you were trying to find an alternative hiding place for the jewels but were disturbed by Cordelia yelling out like that."

"You do need to explain that properly," said Harry. "Saying you were getting a book seems a bit of a poor excuse, seeing as you weren't carrying one."

Inspector Thomas was silently taking everything in, keeping to the back of the room as unobtrusively as he could.

"Well, I fancied none of them if you must know."

Harry winced. "There are all kinds of different genres in the library, George. There must have been something you liked."

Hattie piped up in a small voice. "Harry, didn't you lock the library door that night? You told me you had seen someone roaming about on the landing the night before and had worried for some reason."

"By Jove, you're right Hattie darling," said Harry. "I did lock it, and pocketed the key too."

All eyes turned again to George who was beginning to look defeated.

"I think George and I would like to have a private word with you please, Inspector," said Cordelia in a resigned voice.

"Very well, we will go back to the library. No one is to leave this room. A police officer will be outside the door if you need anything." Inspector Thomas rose and led the way to the door with George and Cordelia following behind.

"So what is it you want to say to me?" asked the inspector when they were seated in the library.

George removed his glasses and put them on the desk and rubbed his eyes wearily. He looked over at Cordelia who began to speak tentatively.

"Well, it's like this. I know you already guessed, but George is my husband."

"So am I to believe that your lying to your own family about your husband's death has good motives behind it?" Inspector Thomas' voice was sharp.

Cordelia looked down at her hands in shame.

"Look here, Inspector," George put his glasses back on and banged his fist on the desk. "You can check me out as much as you like, but you won't find anything dishonest on my record. I am in the business of selling precious jewels and am well known in my field. In my area in America the rich come to me first as they know they will get quality. I am not a thief, nor a murderer for that matter. However, on saying that, the market for jewels has taken a downturn and I was worried that I'd go out of business if things didn't pick up soon.

"One day, while he was in my country, Walter Sinnet got in contact with my company and, ultimately, got through to me. He didn't know I was married to his wife's niece, and I didn't know who he was at first. I sold many items to him and he soon became quite a regular customer. He spent a lot of money and Cordelia and I began to realise the life we had only dreamed of. It wasn't until he had got under my skin, so to speak, and made himself quite a well-known and indispensable customer that he hinted that he wanted cheaper goods. I told you that before."

"There's nothing wrong with wanting cheaper items is there?" Inspector Thomas interrupted George's story.

"No of course not, but the problem was that I found out he was selling them on as the real thing. I wrote to him at once and also spoke to him about it on the telephone, but he just laughed and wouldn't listen. I began to get nervous as my reputation could be on the line. What if people found out, and it was traced back to my company? It could ruin me. I told him so and he made it obvious that he would make sure that I did get the blame instead of him. It was blackmail!"

"The simple thing would have been to stop selling them to him. Why didn't you do that?"

"That's just it. He was spending so much money with me that I could barely afford to let him go. He was buying proper gems along with the paste and paying me more than the going rate for the paste too."

"It was then that he told me about this customer, Inspector, and how concerned he had become about him," said Cordelia, putting her hand over George's hand. "When I found out it was Walter I became angry, we both were and talked for a long time about what to do. In my confusion I started to suspect my own family were treating us like that on purpose. I wasn't sure if Aunt Blanche was involved with the situation or not and got more and more paranoid and mistrustful of her. We decided it best not to let on that we were married. George was to come to England on the pretext of business and I was to be here in the background as a widow. That gave me the excuse to visit and be here for my husband, plus to find out surreptitiously what my aunt was aware of."

George picked up on the tale. "I was on my way to speak to him, Inspector, to tell him he needed to stop or I would talk to my solicitor and, if need be, the police. Cordelia and I had decided on the boat over here, that we would rather have no business than dishonest business.

"Mrs Brewer, I mean Florence, stopped me as I was about to knock on the study door, and asked me to take a look at her jewellery before it was put in the safe. I felt slightly irritated as had summoned up the emotional energy to confront Walter and have it all out with him. However, I went with her and as soon as I saw the jewels, I knew they were ones I had supplied to Walter in the past. I was very upset, and this probably came across as rudeness to Florence but I couldn't hide my feelings. What if Walter blamed me in front of her?" He mopped at his brow with a handkerchief and continued. "Walter was angry when I went to him. He presumed I had travelled to England to offer more second-rate goods to him and had no remorse whatsoever when I told him I recognised Florence's jewels. In fact, he laughed in my face. I told him it had to stop or I would see him in prison, and we ended up shouting at each other I'm afraid."

Inspector Thomas thought the story had a ring of truth to it. "Where had you been, Mr Brown, on the night your wife had an intruder?"

"I was the intruder I'm afraid, Inspector. Sleep evaded me that night as my mind was spinning. Walter had been murdered, and I knew I would be a suspect when the truth came out about my business dealings with him. Plus I had not been honest about Cordelia being my wife. And on top of all that if it came out he was selling my cheaper jewels as expensive ones, I guessed I would be in big trouble. I was convinced we would both hang for his murder and so I waited until I thought everyone would be asleep before creeping into Cordelia's room to wake her up and talk it all through. Unfortunately my wife didn't realise it was me and screamed. In a panic I left the room and ran into Harry and Joseph."

"You must have an opinion on why the jewellery was found in your room, Mr Brown. What is your reasoning?" asked Inspector Thomas in a casual way. "Did you take it and was it your intention to get rid of the evidence when opportunity presented itself?"

"No Inspector, no!" blurted out George vehemently. "I did not touch those jewels and I can't figure out why they were in my room. Someone put them there, though, that's for sure. Somebody wanted to frame me. They are all suspicious of me here. I can feel it. I'd like to think that it was Walter, but I have a feeling he was dead before they were stolen."

He took his glasses off, wiped them with his handkerchief and put them back on, blinking to get his eyes back in focus.

Inspector Thomas turned to Cordelia. "If you were suspicious about your aunt being involved, I expect you would assume it was her that hid the jewels in your husband's room?"

Cordelia gave a little start. "Now I've seen her I can't really believe that she was aware of anything at all. She was fiercely loyal to her husband and I'm sure swept a lot of his foibles under the carpet so to speak, but I don't think she would have stood for this. I don't think he ever told her what he got up to in his business life."

"In that case is there anything else you'd like to tell me?" Inspector Thomas asked gently.

"No," said Cordelia still holding onto George's hand. "There isn't anything else to say. Unless absolutely necessary please would you keep our story quiet until I have spoken to my aunt first?"

"I assure you I will do my best," replied Inspector Thomas. "Please go back to the others now."

He sighed as they left the room. Love the job as he did, it was extremely tedious when people suppressed the truth from him. He decided to go and find James and send him home with one of the gardeners as time was getting on. He rang the bell for the butler and informed him he would be spending the night at Witton Park along with one other policeman and then wandered out to the driveway, deep in thought.

Chapter 18

"Would you like a Gimlet, Florence?" said Rose as she crossed the drawing room to the drinks tray. "I certainly feel like I need one."

"Yes please. I do hope that police inspector sorts it all out soon, as I don't think I can take much more. Right now all I want to do is go home and get my jewels properly valued. Not knowing the truth is making me feel very much on edge. Oh, do forgive me, my dear, I'm being insensitive."

"That's okay. I feel guilty more than anything else, as grief seems to have evaded me. Father and I were simply not close and I can't do anything to change that now. It's a shame, but I just don't feel that sad."

As they were talking, Hattie came in and smiled at them. "I hope I'm not interrupting anything private?" she said.

"No of course you're not. Have a drink, Hattie."

"Thank you, something soft please."

Rose handed a glass of fruit juice to her and then sniffed hard. "Gosh, what a strong smell of smoke!"

"It's the bonfire outside," said Hattie crossing to the window and looking out. "The window's open a little bit. I'll shut it." She pulled the window shut and fastened it.

The bonfire was still going strong and crackled away merrily, devouring the chopped up tree that was being fed to it. Inspector Thomas watched it for a while, enjoying the warmth, and then looked around for James. He was nowhere to be seen.

"Has anyone seen where my son has got to?" he called out to the gardeners who were tidying up their tools for the day.

"No Sir," said one of them, taking his cap off and sauntering up to the inspector. "Haven't seen him for some time now. He might have got a lift back to the village with one of the police officers that were here."

"Well yes I can't say I would blame him," smiled Inspector Thomas. "I have been here a long time and there's only so much exploring a boy can do! I wish he'd told me though."

Putting his hands in his pockets he turned around and wandered off down the drive to get some air and take a look around. In a few short moments he found himself down by the lake, taking in its splendour. No one would have known this had been artificially engineered at Witton Park and completed within the last few months. It looked like it had always been there. Marvellous! He sauntered off around the path to the right of the lake, away from the boathouse. The freshness of the wind seemed to breeze through his mind, reviving his thoughts, and he tried to stop himself focussing on the investigation for a few minutes.

Before long he was out of sight of the house and, sticking to the path, followed its course around the lake, through some tall trees, and up a steadily increasing incline. It was muddy, but that didn't worry him and he continued to march onwards. He could hear the roar of water in the distance as he began to climb the hill path, leaving everything behind him. It wasn't long before he was panting but he forged ahead. It seemed as if he must be ascending the top of a very high cliff.

Banks of rhododendron bushes prevented him from seeing the view of the water but he continued on his journey, enjoying the exercise. He vaguely wondered if James had explored this part of the estate, but there were no other imprints of shoes in the muddy ground.

The steep path stopped abruptly and Inspector Thomas found himself on a grassy plateau opposite an ornate carved wooden bench facing towards the lake below. It looked as if a chunk of the thick bushes had been cut out to make a space for the bench, for on either side of it there was no way of seeing the view. The sound of the thundering water was quite loud by now and, panting slightly from his exertions, he apprehensively walked over to the bench and looked over the edge, holding onto the back of it for support.

The panorama that revealed itself to him was incredible, and he was glad he had something solid to hang onto. It was definitely not a sight for anyone suffering from vertigo.

Inspector Thomas watched in awe as torrents of water plunged over the side of a higher plateau and fell into a lake below it, swirling and raging around in anguish while a wall of water vapour rose into the air, as if it were trying to make its way back to where it had come from. It looked violent and angry.

An immense statue rose hauntingly up out of the lake, reminding him of the stories he had read as a small boy of mythical creatures coming out of the deep. White foamy water bubbled and gurgled angrily out of the mouth of the giant marble dolphin head and screamed its way over the side into the vast depths of the lake below it. Something moaned from deep underneath the water sounding much like the groaning of a sinking ship.

All at once, Inspector Thomas felt fear. He knew it wasn't rational, but he turned tail and fled back down the path, slipping and sliding in the mud. He hurried back towards the house not caring if he fell or not. The house was further than he had thought, but at last, as he saw the boathouse come into view, he slowed down, feeling a little ashamed of himself. Afraid of a bit of water indeed! He took a deep breath and composed himself, waiting until the pounding of his heart in his head began to slow back down to an acceptable pace.

Once back at the boathouse he was hailed by a voice and turned round to see Harry coming towards him. "Taking in the view, Inspector? Beautiful isn't it? Shame you're seeing it under such horrible circumstances."

"Yes. I was just thinking to myself that it is a wonder of modern design. It must have taken a lot of hard work." Inspector Thomas was surprised at how calm his own voice sounded in his ears, but was grateful for it.

"An awful lot of hard work! The folly was built first and the lake came later. Unfortunately a labourer died when a steel girder fell on him. The poor guy had been telling my father it wasn't safe, but he was ignored. That was Father all over, I'm afraid. He just did things his own way and took no notice of anyone else. It's tragic."

"Very," muttered Inspector Thomas.

"Well, I must get back to the house. None of us feel we can go back to the folly after the other night's shock. I merely came down here to make sure the police had locked up properly."

He threw the key up into the air, caught it, and put it in his pocket. He then disappeared back up the path whistling and Inspector Thomas watched him go.

In the distance he could see Blanche and Aubrey strolling arm in arm on the terrace looking content and happy in each other's company.

He ambled back up the path and, as he sidestepped the rhododendrons, he noticed Florence slipping into the French windows at the side of the house.

Before dinner, Cordelia approached Blanche and asked if she could have a private word with her. Looking surprised Blanche agreed at once and put her arm through Cordelia's, taking her across the hall to her husband's study. "We'll be quite alone in here, my dear. Whatever is the matter? You look terribly worried."

"Aunt Blanche, I'm afraid I have a confession to make to you."

"If you've come to confess to Walter's murder, I forgive you already," smiled Blanche jokingly, then her face took on a more serious expression when Cordelia didn't smile back.

"I didn't mean to be flippant. All this is so dramatic I made a tasteless joke to lighten the atmosphere. Silly me, please continue."

"I'm afraid I haven't been honest with you. I don't even know where to start but, in a nutshell, my husband hasn't died. I lied to you all and he is very much alive."

Blanche gave a little start. "Alive?"

"Yes, and what's more, he's here in this house. My husband is George Brown."

"My goodness Cordelia, are you being serious?"

"Yes. Walter was putting him and the business in a difficult position and he wanted to come and confront him. I'm sorry to say that I suspected you could be in on it too, and so I lied to you. I know now that you had nothing to do with it and you couldn't possibly have. I'm so terribly ashamed."

Blanche gave her a quick hug and then held her at arm's length, looking into her face. "No need to apologise, my dear. I understand. Of course, I knew Walter wasn't honest in his business dealings, but I always kept out of it. He wouldn't have listened to me if I'd tried to tame him, but if I had known he was upsetting you I would have interfered at once. Perhaps I should have tried. I was wrong too and I apologise for that. I realise now I should have taken more of a stand with him, so tell me what it was that he did exactly."

"I'm sure you can imagine. Don't blame yourself; it's not your fault. We can only be responsible for our own actions and not the actions of those around us."

"Yes, but I wish I'd been aware. It's strange to think of you and your husband doing business with him. I'm sure you had your reasons for it, but why were you doing business with him in the first place?"

"George didn't know who he was. It wasn't until he began to get upset that he talked to me about it and I obviously knew Walter's name and put two and two together."

"Oh dear. Why don't you go and fetch that husband of yours and introduce me properly? You can both tell me all about it then and afterwards we'll go and let the others know your news."

Chapter 19

After dinner that evening, the whole household gathered in the drawing room. The men, including Inspector Thomas, were playing cards at the table and the women were sitting around in the comfortable chairs. The underlying atmosphere was strained despite the cheery conversation that floated about in the room. No one had been completely surprised or bothered by George and Cordelia's news and nothing much was said about it, although Florence had a few choice words to throw into the conversation.

Blanche was embroidering and Hattie was sitting next to her, trying to learn some new stitches.

"Oh you are clever, Mrs Sinnet. I hope to be as good as you before long. If I keep practising I'm sure to improve. Mother isn't creative so all I've learned I've had to find out for myself."

"Come up anytime my dear," replied Blanche snipping at her thread. "Rose isn't interested in embroidery so I'd love to take you under my wing and pass this art on to someone. Besides the finished product, it's such a relaxing and therapeutic thing to do."

"Mother! You make it sound as if I'm a complete imbecile," huffed Rose, turning round from the conversation she was having with Cordelia about George. "I love learning things from you. I'm just not very creative, that's all."

"I know, Rose, and I wouldn't want you forcing yourself to do something for my benefit," said Blanche in a soothing voice. "The truth is I wouldn't change you for the world as you well know, so just carry on being yourself."

Slightly pacified, Rose gave her mother a small smile and stood up. "Oh, I am bored being stuck in here," she said hobbling across the room to stretch her legs.

"Is there something wrong with your shoes, darling?" asked Blanche watching her.

"Just a couple of rather vicious blisters on the backs of my ankles," said Rose, glancing down at her shoes. "They are a bit sore actually. I think I need some new shoes."

"Well, as soon as this nightmare is over, we will go shopping together and get you some new ones. It seems a bit strange that they'd give you blisters now though, you've been wearing them comfortably for ages."

"I know. Anyway, Father complains when we go shopping. Oh," she stopped short. "I guess we can go shopping whenever we want to now, can't we?"

"Yes, we certainly can, and there will be no guilt in it." Blanche sounded sterner than she had intended to, and lightened it with a smile. She looked around at the others. "I guess it sounds mercenary, talking about shopping when Walter has just died. It's funny the things one thinks of at a time of crisis."

Aubrey looked at her over his hand of cards. "No one thinks anything negative of you. You're a kind and thoughtful woman and you're taking care of the needs of your children."

Harry laughed. "Grown up children, Aubrey! You make us sound like we're little toddlers. We don't really need taking care of now."

"Really Harry?" Blanche waggled her finger at her son in a friendly manner. "You get so lost in your books that you forget to come to meals half the time."

"So you are assured of an inheritance then?" asked Florence turning to look at Blanche.

"Not a very sensitive thing to say my dear," said Joseph going red.

"I didn't mean to be insensitive," retorted Florence in surprise. "I merely meant that no one actually knows what is in Walter's will yet, or do they?"

"I'm not about to share the contents of my husband's will Florence, but rest assured this family is fine."

Rose made her way over to the piano and lifted the lid. She idly played a few bars, then sat down at the stool and began to play a haunting tune, her fingers racing unrestrainedly up and down the keys as if in despair.

Cordelia felt as if the music was putting her into a trance. It was hypnotic, wild, and dramatic. She shook herself as if to break the spell and forced herself to talk to Florence about the storm.

"It was simply terrifying," Florence said. "Joseph just slept through the whole thing; strange as he is usually such a light sleeper."

Inspector Thomas glanced thoughtfully at Joseph who was frowning over his hand of cards.

"I'm afraid the wind's picking up again," said Harry as a breeze swept under the door and lifted the edge of the rug. "We may well be in for another bad night."

"Surely not as bad as the other night?" said Aubrey getting up from the table and opening the curtains so they could all see out. It was dark outside, but the moon was bright and shone down on the front lawn illuminating the dark bushes and casting strange shadows across it. The bonfire was still alight, although much smaller than it had been, and threw its colourful glow over the milky white statue of Athena. Orange flecks floated up into the sky and disappeared.

"Thankfully no, I think that was the storm to end all storms."

Rose thundered up and down the piano keys and the tune ended abruptly; silence hanging heavily in the air. She got up and hobbled back down the room to sit with the others as if exhausted.

Suddenly there was a loud bang, and a face appeared at the window, hands clutching at the frame. It was a young boy and his face was set in a mask of terror and mixed with mud and streaks of red blood. Florence gave out an unearthly high-pitched scream and clutched at Cordelia's arm making her almost jump out of her skin too. Blanche gave a little yelp and staggered backwards while Rose and Hattie grabbed each other's hands in fright. The men all sprung to their feet, chairs screeching across the parquet flooring, and bounded over the rug across the room to the window. Not as fast as Inspector Thomas, though, who had recognised the face of his son.

He opened the window and half dragged, half carried, James into the room. Poor James was dazed, in shock and terrifyingly pale.

"Quick, help me," ordered a shaken Inspector Thomas, loosening James' shirt at the neck and then rubbing his cold hands. Aubrey picked up James' legs and George grabbed him under the arms. They carried him to the chaise longue and gently placed him there, dragging it closer to the fire.

Harry rang for the butler who almost instantly appeared at his side. "Hot sweet tea, quick!" The butler, who for once was not composed, rushed off to fetch it.

Gladys, who had come in to see what was happening, dragged a blanket off one of the chairs and placed it over the little lad's trembling body and Hattie began to wipe the worst of the mud off his face with her handkerchief.

They all clamoured around the chaise longue, talking and questioning him in loud voices.

"Hush do," said Rose almost violently. "The poor boy is quite overwrought. Give him some space."

A sudden gust of wind made the window crash shut making everyone jump again.

Aubrey fastened it and drew the curtains.

Soon the tea arrived and James sat up, leaning on his elbow, sipping at the hot liquid, and beginning to feel slightly more revived. He looked at his father and tears began to pour down his dirty little face.

"What happened, my boy?" asked Inspector Thomas tenderly. "I thought you had gone home. Have you been here the whole time?"

James nodded mutely.

"Did someone hurt you?" Inspector Thomas was peering at the wound on top of James' head, where the blood had congealed in his hair.

"I found something; a clue Father," stuttered James. A gun. I found a gun in the rhododendron bushes."

Everyone gasped.

"You found what?" Inspector Thomas' voice rang out like a pistol shot. "Where is it?"

He glanced around at everyone, trying to make out facial expressions.

"It's gone. I'd put it in my pocket but it isn't in there now." He patted his empty pockets. "Someone slugged me on the back of the head and then pushed me into the bushes. Everything went black, and I passed out. You can't imagine how scary it was. I came to but was dazed and frightened the person was still about. It's obvious they wanted to kill me." His voice wobbled with emotion.

"Are you sure you were hit, dear?" asked Blanche getting down on her knees beside him. "You couldn't possible have tripped and fallen?"

"No!" said James fury rising up from the very depths of his being at the thought of not being believed. "I tell you I was hit, then pushed and was out for the count for a long time. When I came to I was dizzy. I felt about for the gun, but it had gone, so I got up and staggered to the house. When I saw the curtains open and the light streaming out of the window I somehow willed my legs to continue walking as I hoped I would find my father here."

A hush descended on the room and James glared defiantly round at everyone, daring someone to defy him.

"I need to get you cleaned up," said Inspector Thomas eventually, pulling himself together. "Do you think you can walk?"

James nodded and slowly got to his feet, swaying on his wobbly legs. Leaning against his father, who put his arm around him, he hopped across the room to the door and they went out together.

"The gun… he must have found the gun that shot Walter," said Cordelia. "Suddenly this all feels terribly real." She got up and went over to George's side, and he put his hand up to her face and smoothed her hair gently over one ear.

Chapter 20

Upstairs, Inspector Thomas was tucking James up in the bed that had been meant for him, having first cleaned him up a bit. Gladys was dressing the wound on his head.

"There now my duck," she cooed as he winced at her touch. "Just stay here in bed and I'll get you something to eat. You look as if you need it." James smiled at her gratefully.

"I need to sort this out, my boy," said Inspector Thomas, heaving himself up off the side of the bed. "I'm going downstairs to find out who did this to you. Keep the bedroom door locked and don't let anyone in unless it is Gladys or myself, do you hear me?"

"Yes Father," James spoke in a tired voice. "It's unlikely that anyone will try to get me again anyway. They were just after the gun and were probably worried about their fingerprints being on it. I expect it's at the bottom of the lake by now."

Inspector Thomas smiled fondly down at his son and left the room, once again reminding James to lock it after him. He waited until he heard the key click behind him and then descended the stairs.

He strode into the drawing room and took control. "Right, everyone sit down. We are going to talk."

Everyone sat dutifully down and looked at the inspector expectantly.

"My son and I had lunch together and then he went back outside. I went looking for him late afternoon and the gardeners informed me they hadn't seen him for some time and he had probably got a lift home with another officer. Needless to say, he did not go home. I need to know where you all were after lunch. Let's start with you, Mr Brown, seeing as you are sitting closest to me."

George looked up. "Well, let's see, I was in the drawing room with the rest of the household after lunch, and then went to the

113

library with Cordelia and you to talk. I didn't step foot out of the house at all. Neither of us did." He looked at Cordelia who gazed back and nodded in agreement.

"Mrs Brewer?" Inspector Thomas turned to Florence next.

"I was in the drawing room. You had found my jewels and I was looking them over thoroughly, making sure they weren't damaged. I did not go near your son, nor even know where he was." She sniffed.

"Did you go outside at all, Mrs Brewer?"

"Certainly not."

"Are you sure of that?" The inspector's voice sounded like a pistol shot.

"Well of course I am," said Florence indignantly.

"How strange, for I happened to be down by the lake, and on my return I saw you going into the house Mrs Brewer." The inspector's voice had a hard edge to it. All eyes turned to Florence.

"Well you must be mistaken, I did not go outside. Oh, wait a minute, you're right; I stepped outside of the French windows for a few seconds late afternoon, just to breathe in some fresh air. I did not go 'outside' as such. Most of the time I was in the drawing room talking to Rose, isn't that right Rose?"

Rose nodded. "Yes, it's true Inspector. We were inside talking together in this very room. I left for a few minutes only myself to fetch something from my room."

Aubrey spoke up. "Blanche and I went outside together to take in some air this afternoon. We sat down on a bench overlooking the lake for a while, and then meandered around the terrace. I didn't see anyone at all, did you dear, apart from the gardeners and the inspector himself? Oh hang on, we saw Harry briefly, didn't we?"

"Yes, we saw Harry walking along the path to the lake," said Blanche. "He spoke to us for a few seconds, to say he was going to make sure the folly was locked up, and he was only gone a few minutes. Not enough time to knock your son out and dispose of a gun, Inspector."

"How long do you think it takes to knock someone on the head then Mrs Sinnet?"

"Well, I couldn't say really," faltered Blanche.

"I was with you, Inspector, when the jewels were found," said Harry quickly. "Then I was in the library on my own, until I remembered about the folly. I went straight there, seeing my mother and Aubrey on the way, and then I ran into you at the lake. Mother's right, there was no time to bash someone over the head like that."

"It only takes seconds to hit someone," replied the inspector staring at Harry distrustfully. "You could easily have thrown the gun into the lake around the time you were there talking to me."

"No. I stand by what I said. The timing of seeing him, hitting him, disposing of the gun, and running into you, remaining calm the whole time, would not be possible."

"What was the reason for you locking the folly door anyway? Who would want to go there again after the horrific discovery of your father's body? Also, if anyone had wanted to go there, what would be the problem? There's nothing to hide in the folly is there, nothing worth stealing?"

"It was purely force of habit, and something to do to take my mind off everything for a few minutes. Father liked the door to be locked and besides, the gun cabinet is in there."

Pericles jumped off the windowsill startling everyone.

"Miss Abberton?" All eyes turned to Hattie.

"I was here in the drawing room, sitting looking out of the window on the lake side. I saw you and Harry talking in the distance, and I saw Blanche and Aubrey taking a turn across the terrace. I was quietly practising embroidery all afternoon and didn't move from my place at all. If you like I can show you my progress if you need the proof."

"Actually Hattie, that's not quite right," piped up Florence. "I distinctly remember you coming in when Rose and I were having a drink. Do you remember, Rose?"

"Yes, now you mention it," replied Rose thoughtfully. "I had said there was a smell of smoke, and you shut the window. You only arrived in the drawing room then."

"That's right," faltered Hattie. "I was in my bedroom for a short time choosing from the threads that Blanche had given to me, but I came straight down here and did not go anywhere else afterwards." She looked imploringly at Harry.

"Leave her alone," he said to the room in general. "Hattie isn't likely to go about knocking small boys on the head. This is ridiculous."

"You say so, Sir, but someone did just that," snapped back Inspector Thomas. "We are going to get to the bottom of this mystery tonight."

There was a small tap on the door and the butler appeared over the threshold. "Police headquarters on the phone for you, Sir."

A few minutes later Inspector Thomas returned to the drawing room having had an illuminating conversation with headquarters.

"We have confirmation that the doctor who met Mr Sinnet at the house party has said he did indeed think there was a case of consumption there."

Blanche bowed her head slightly.

"We also can confirm that Mr Marlin has been at his house with his wife the entire weekend."

"Mr Marlin?" questioned Rose. "You didn't suspect him, did you? He's a lovely old man."

"I have no choice but to suspect everyone I'm afraid, Miss Sinnet. Right, let's talk fingerprints. The murderer had to have gone to the gun cabinet in the folly to remove the gun that shot Walter. The weather has been too extreme for that person to return to the folly to get rid of any fingerprint evidence…"

"Not quite so, Inspector." Joseph spoke up. "Three men were in the folly putting Walter's body there once he had been brought up out of his watery grave. There would have been plenty of time to wipe off any offending prints. Sorry, chaps," he added to Harry, George and Aubrey as an afterthought, putting his monocle in and glancing round.

George sighed heavily. "When is this nightmare going to end?"

"Anyway," continued Inspector Thomas. "The murderer shot Walter, threw the gun into the rhododendrons and then saw James messing about there and had to intervene. According to headquarters, the only fingerprints on the cabinet belonged to Mrs Sinnet."

Blanche gasped. "That's because I shut the glass door. It had swung open when we all went to the folly. Someone must surely have seen that and remembered me doing so? The murderer must have already shot my husband by then and wiped the cabinet clean of prints if mine were the only ones there. That goes to show it was a premeditated crime." She looked imploringly round at the others hoping to find someone to believe her.

"What about Aubrey then?" Joseph sang out in a reckless manner. "He went looking for Walter when Florence's jewels were discovered missing. Nobody went to the folly with him; he was alone and could have wiped away the evidence. He could have killed Walter right there and then in fact. He could even have disposed of the body in that time."

Aubrey raised his eyebrows and looked at Joseph, shaking his head slightly. "I did not kill Walter, old son. You're barking up the wrong tree. Anyway, if I had, there would have been ample time for me to wipe any prints off the gun and dispose of that properly too."

Joseph slumped back in his chair, defeated.

"A police constable is searching the house again at my order," said Inspector Thomas. "He is looking for the gun. However, I suspect it is probably at the bottom of the lake by now. No one in their right mind would bring it in the house unless they were going to try and frame someone. I asked him to look for footprints on the muddy path around by the rhododendrons when I was taking James upstairs, but unfortunately there were too many of them, as we have all walked down there recently. It was also too dark for him to see properly even with his flashlight. I'd like you all to turn out your pockets and bags now for me please."

A low murmur of complaint sounded out, but everyone reluctantly showed the inspector what was on them, which didn't amount to very much. Florence had her powder compact and a startling red lipstick in her bag. Hattie had some thread and a handkerchief, and George had his glasses case and the loupe that he always carried to inspect gemstones. The others had various small items and a handful of coins. The inspector continued to talk.

"By the way, I haven't heard from you yet, Mr Brewer. You have made some wild accusations against people, but you haven't told me of your whereabouts this afternoon."

"I say, Inspector, don't start suspecting me," said Joseph in a high voice. "I was in my room having a lie down as I had a nasty headache. There was way too much stress for my liking. Gladys knocked on the door and came in briefly to see if I wanted a cup of tea. I said yes, and she went and brought one up. She also appeared a little later to take the cup and saucer back downstairs. You can check with her if you like."

"Don't worry I will do," replied the inspector sighing. "I don't suppose you looked out of your window at all while you were upstairs? Your bedroom faces the lake does it not?"

"I can't say I did, I'm afraid. I lay down with a cool flannel on my forehead most of the time."

"Inspector, what about the person who my father was arguing with on the telephone?" said Rose. "Harry told us he was threatening Father. Could he have somehow got here and murdered him?"

Before he had a chance to reply, there was a little rap at the drawing room door and a police officer's head appeared round it. Inspector Thomas went out to talk to him in the hall.

"Do you think he's found the gun?" said Blanche to the room in general. They all started to talk at once, speculating on the evening's events. In the middle of their conversations the inspector came in again.

"No gun so far I'm afraid," he said looking at their expectant faces and guessing what they were thinking. "However, it's quite interesting that a certain someone's shoes have fresh wet mud splashed on them when they weren't like that earlier on in the day, according to the butler. Maybe that person would like to tell me what they were doing outside today when they said they were inside the whole time?"

They all looked silently around at each other, wondering whom it was that the inspector was talking about. The sound of the clock ticking on the mantelpiece seemed to take on a surreal tone as if the very heart of it was beating loudly and echoing everyone else's.

118

"I'm waiting." Inspector Thomas' voice was loud, interrupting the clock's tick that was somnolent in its rhythm.

Still no one spoke.

"Who do you mean, Inspector?" twittered Joseph. "Tell us."

Gradually all eyes turned to look at the person Inspector Thomas was staring at. Hattie. She turned scared eyes up to him and backed herself up against the back of a chair, leaning on it.

"I did go out, it's true. I didn't want to tell you because I knew I hadn't done anything wrong, but didn't want to be considered a suspect." Her voice came out in a rush.

"Everyone is a suspect as you very well know. You had the opportunity to tell us earlier, Miss Abberton. When Miss Sinnet and Mrs Brewer said you went into the drawing room a smell of smoke came in with you. You shut the window saying it was from the bonfire, but in actual fact the smoke was coming from you, wasn't it?"

Hattie swallowed, looking fearful. "Yes, I was near the bonfire having a quick look at it. I couldn't bear being cooped up any longer."

"But there was nothing wrong in going out. You hadn't been forbidden to do so, so why try and pull the blanket over our eyes? Admitting to being outside wouldn't automatically mean you had hit James over the head. The bonfire is fairly near the rhododendron bushes, isn't it?" snapped Inspector Thomas.

"Yes not too far, but I didn't go to them and I certainly didn't hurt your son, I swear."

"Well, I put it to you that you did. The mud on your shoes is consistent with the mud around the bushes, not the mud from the drive, which is different altogether. Would you like to explain that?"

Hattie began to shake. Harry went over to her and put his arm defiantly around her.

"Leave her alone, for goodness' sake," he half-shouted. "Can't you see the poor girl is upset?" Hattie looked up at him gratefully.

"Mr Sinnet. Harry," said the inspector in a weary voice. "It was you, wasn't it that told me today that a worker from the village was killed here by a steel girder? Your father couldn't have cared less that there was danger on site. He wanted his folly and lake dream realised, and it didn't matter to him that a man died. What was the name of that man?"

"I think it was Baker," said Harry looking surprised. "Was that his name Mother?"

Blanche nodded weakly.

"Baker? How interesting. Why have you given us a false name, Miss Abberton? Or should I say Miss Baker? That man was your father, wasn't it?" He pointed at Hattie.

Everyone gasped and Hattie paled even further. She looked around at everyone and gulped.

"Yes. It was my father," she was defiant. "He told Mr Sinnet over and over that the steel work was unsafe, but nothing was done about it. He said that someone would be killed, but we never thought it would be him." She began to sob in earnest as Harry's eyes widened in alarm.

"Mr Sinnet did nothing to stop his death... and he could have prevented it. He did nothing to help mother and me once he had died either, despite us pleading for help. It sickened me to plead, but mother said we had no choice. We had hardly any money so I came here to shame him in front of his family, but when I arrived I lost my nerve. I'm sorry I lied about my name."

"You shot him in cold blood!"

"I didn't! Please believe me. It's true I wasn't unhappy that someone did kill him, but it wasn't me, I swear. It was more in my interest to have him alive so that I could try to get help for my mother and me. It wasn't fair, Mother spent her life helping others and doing good works in the village, but when it came to our turn needing help, no one was interested."

"I'm putting it to you that you took the gun from the gun cabinet, you cleaned your prints off the glass, you shot Mr Sinnet at the side of the lake, and then you threw the gun in the bushes. When my son started messing about too close to the weapon, you rushed outside and hit him on the head. Isn't that correct?"

"No. NO!"

"Why were you by the rhododendrons this afternoon?"

"I wasn't. I tell you, I went near the bonfire only. I can't account for the mud on my shoes, but I did not go down the path to the bushes at all." She turned to Harry imploring him to believe her. "I didn't kill your father," she said to him quietly.

"It doesn't look good but I believe you," he said, an uneasy look crossing his face.

"Did you see anyone else outside?" asked Inspector Thomas, changing tactic.

Hattie thought hard, her forehead wrinkling up. "No. I'm afraid I didn't."

Inspector Thomas circled the room, thinking hard.

Blanche went to Hattie and handed her a handkerchief, patting her lightly on the arm as Harry put his arm around her and gave her a little squeeze.

The inspector started talking again. "We'll come back to you in a minute, Miss Abberton. I will continue to call you Abberton for the time being as we are all used to the name. Let's go back to the theft of Mrs Brewer's jewels. You said you hid them in your wardrobe, Mrs Brewer?"

"I did indeed, Inspector. There were quite a few boxes and cases and so I put them on the floor of the wardrobe and put a cloth on top to camouflage their hiding place."

"Was your bedroom door open when you hid them? Did anyone see you hide them away? A guest? A maid? Anyone?" asked Inspector Thomas, still circling the room and looking at no one in particular.

"No, nobody. Well, apart from Joseph of course."

"Ah yes, Mr Brewer." The inspector stopped walking and turned to Joseph, who was looking uncomfortable. "You seem to be the only person who knew where the jewels were, Mr Brewer. How interesting."

"Why interesting, Inspector?" said Joseph feigning ignorance.

"I think you took those jewels, Mr Brewer. You desperately needed money, and when Mr Brown told your wife the jewels were worthless you hatched a plan. You decided to pretend they had been stolen so that you could claim the insurance money on them."

"That is not so," retorted Joseph haughtily.

"So, I see it like this. You decided to get rid of the jewels and you took them and hid them somewhere on the night of the murder. For some reason you had no opportunity to get rid of them there and then. Perhaps the storm prevented you doing so. You crept along the corridor the next night and saw Mr Brown's bedroom door open. He had gone in to talk to his wife who had not yet woken up. You saw an opportunity and shoved the jewels under his wardrobe and as you heard her scream, you raced back to your room and made it look as if you had just got up."

"Very inventive I'm sure, but simply not true," said Joseph obstinately. "I just woke up at the scream and went straight to the door."

"Actually Jo," said Harry thinking back. "When Cordelia yelled out like that, I was out of bed in a heartbeat. I raced to the door and found that you had got to your door before me. I thought that strange at the time."

Florence turned to her husband. "In general, Jo, you are usually such a light sleeper so I don't question your getting up so quickly. However, the night of the murder, the storm was horrendous. I spoke to you to see if you were asleep and you didn't answer, you were out like a light. Extraordinary!" She put her hand up to her mouth in sudden horror, realising she was implicating him by accident.

"Maybe he didn't answer because he wasn't in bed," said Inspector Thomas sharply.

"I fell asleep in the library on the night my father was killed," said Harry quickly. "When I awoke the storm was in full force and I heard someone running down the upstairs corridor by the illumination of the lightning strike outside the window. I called out, but the person didn't answer. Was that you, Jo?"

"No it wasn't, thank you very much, Harry." Joseph had a pained expression on his face.

"Things are not looking too good for you I'm afraid, Mr Brewer," said Inspector Thomas. "Not only were you short of money, but you were also extremely angry with Walter Sinnet for treating you badly, and your father before you. I suggest you tell us the truth. I'm going to go and check on my son and then I'm coming back to hear what you have to say."

Chapter 21

James was fast asleep and snoring gently when the inspector went upstairs to see him. Gladys was just leaving the room with an empty plate and gave the inspector the room key for him to lock up if he deemed it necessary.

"He's going to be fine, Sir. Bless him. It'll be a good story to tell the children when he goes back to school. He's eaten like a horse and his colour has returned to his cheeks, so don't you fret about him."

Gladys disappeared down the back stairs that led to the kitchen and the inspector went down the main staircase to join the others, leaving the bedroom door unlocked.

Back in the drawing room, Joseph was looking panic-stricken and kept fiddling with his monocle chain.

"Right then, Mr Brewer, let's hear what you've got to say," said the inspector perching himself on the edge of an armchair and getting out his notepad and pencil.

"Well, I didn't take those jewels," Joseph said stubbornly. "I slept through the storm, but I woke up at Cordelia's scream the following night. That's all there is to it. You're right in the fact that I was angry and I also have no money, but I am not a thief or a killer. I don't know how to prove that to you."

"So, let's get this straight. Only you and your wife knew that the jewels were hidden where they were. You told no one about them, and no one saw you hide them. In essence everyone thought you had given them to Gladys to put in the safe." He turned to Blanche. "Mrs Sinnet, can you vouch for the honesty of your servants?"

"Oh yes, Inspector," said Blanche fervently. "They've all been with us for years and we have never had any problems with them. Honest as the day is long, they are."

"Then, one of you two took the jewels." Inspector Thomas pointed at the Brewers accusingly. "If it wasn't you, Mr Brewer, then it must have been your wife."

Florence gasped. "Steal my own jewels? You must be mad!"

"You woke up and called out to your husband to see if he was awake. No answer. You took your chance and got out of bed and gathered up the jewels in a pillowcase and hid them somewhere where you thought they wouldn't be detected. That hiding place was in Mr Brown's bedroom. That was a brave thing to do because you didn't know if he was awake or not, and chances were that he would be awake, with all the noise of the storm."

Florence looked obstinate and said nothing.

"It would be better for you to admit it, Mrs Brewer. I have enough on my plate trying to solve a murder without trying to solve a fictitious theft too."

Florence continued to look mutinous.

"This is your last chance and it is in your best interest to speak truthfully. Do you want to tell me about it now, or down at the station?" said Inspector Thomas in his most official sounding voice, which rang with authority. "If you continue to lie, things will not go well for you."

Florence burst into tears at once. "Okay, okay," she said holding her hands up in surrender. "I will talk. What you've said is true. I wouldn't have admitted it but I didn't want you getting into trouble for me, Joseph." She looked mournfully at her husband. "I was angry with Mr Brown for telling me that all the jewels I owned were fakes and my only thought was to get rid of the jewels and claim for them on the insurance.

"Joseph was upset that Walter had suddenly changed his mind about the investment. That must have been because he knew the jewels were fakes seeing as he bought them in the first place. There was no money in them so how could he take them as payment?" She took a breath. "I wanted to get rid of them properly; perhaps throw them in the lake, but the storm was raging and I couldn't go outside in it. I was in the corridor thinking, when I heard the sound of footsteps coming up the stairs. In a panic I ran and hid behind the curtains at the end.

"Harry passed by and went into his bedroom, so I left them hidden in the suit of armour standing by the curtains and slipped back to my room. I had no intention of implicating George. Later in the night, because I couldn't sleep, I went to get them but sensed I wasn't the only one up and about, so I quietly opened the nearest door, which happened to be George's room. I slid the pillowcase under the wardrobe, which is right next to the door, and went back to my room. Later I heard the tree fall, and then there were more footsteps and I heard George call out to someone downstairs. I now know that was Harry and Aubrey, and they were sorting out the problem with the front door. That is the whole truth, Inspector."

Joseph had been staring, open-mouthed at his wife. "Darling," he said eventually, grasping her hand. "I didn't realise you were quite so worried and I am sorry I've been such a bounder. From the moment we get home, if we ever get home, I am going to get a job and look after you properly." He dabbed at Florence's eyes with the handkerchief she was holding. They smiled watery smiles at each other.

George, however, was not smiling. "This is not good enough," he fumed, pushing his glasses up onto the bridge of his nose and frowning at Florence. "I could have been arrested for theft. I came to this country with good intentions so that people like you would not be cheated anymore. This is how I am repaid?" He paced the room looking much like a thundercloud.

Cordelia spoke up. "Well, I must say I'm not very impressed Florence. I thought you were a better woman than that. I should have listened to my inner first impressions of you."

Florence opened her mouth to speak but Inspector Thomas intervened. "I appreciate your honesty, although it is a little late, Mrs Brewer." His tone hardened. "Mr Brown is right. He could have been arrested for theft, and you ultimately could have been charged with insurance fraud."

"I wouldn't have let it go that far," said Florence looking imploringly at George. "I really am sorry. Desperation drove me to it."

"May I add my apologies too?" asked Blanche. "My husband was not good to you and I would like to pay back every single bit of money you spent on those rotten jewels. Just tell me how much and I will give it back to you before you leave Witton Park."

"My constable will take the jewels for a second opinion tomorrow," said the inspector. "They will be valued in the village by the local jeweller and brought back again."

George raised his hands up in frustration.

"So, one mystery solved then," said Aubrey. "Can we get to the bottom of the other before bed? It looks like we're in for a long night." He went over to the sideboard and took the lid off the decanter. "Brandy anyone?" He poured himself a stiff measure and gulped it back before pouring another.

"I would like to take you back to the night of the murder," said Inspector Thomas with authority. "You all had a reason to get rid of Mr Sinnet. I'm going to come to you next, Mrs Brown." He turned to Cordelia who looked up with a start.

"I'm listening, Inspector." She held her head high.

"You came in from outside, wet through, and had to get a bath filled for you."

"And?"

"And I put it to you, and the room, that you had gone back to the folly. You somehow got Walter to the edge of the lake. Perhaps you asked him to take a stroll with you? You shot him and pushed him in, then came back to the house pretending you had just been out for a short walk."

"I see your point, Inspector, but why would Walter agree to a stroll with me when the wind was raging and the rain lashing down? Also when would I have managed to remove the gun from the gun cabinet without him noticing? It makes little sense, I'm afraid, and would not stand up in court."

The inspector paced the room again, thinking hard.

"There are many different ways to achieve your goal. You could have got the gun from the cabinet on the pretext of looking at it for interest's sake. Walter sounded like a man who liked to show off his possessions."

"Anyway, I was with you and George most of the afternoon today, so when would I have got the chance to nip out and bang your son over the head? You're barking up the wrong tree here."

"Mr Sapping?" Aubrey looked up as the inspector spoke his name. "You were the first to leave the folly, but that means nothing. You could have returned at any time."

"Yes, but that doesn't make me a murderer as well you know."

"You could have easily taken the gun, walked Walter to the edge of the lake with it poking in his back, pulled the trigger, and watched him fall in. You could have thrown the gun in the bushes on the way back."

"If that were true, Inspector, I would have got the gun back the next morning when I volunteered to go and look for Walter at the folly. I would then have thrown it in the lake or disposed of it properly. Anyway, if I had shot him, I would have thrown the gun into the lake immediately, not into an overgrown bush."

"Maybe you thought the rhododendron bush was disposing of it properly?"

"Why would I think that? The gardeners would be cutting it back soon. The bushes were properly overgrown and ready for a good chop." Aubrey was batting back words as if they were in a game of verbal tennis.

"You had motive and opportunity."

"Well, it all seems a bit obvious don't you think? If I had wanted to murder the old man I would have done it in a more subtle way. I certainly wouldn't have left myself open to suspicion in this way."

"That would be true if it was a premeditated murder."

"Are you suggesting a crime of passion?" said Aubrey in disgust.

"I'm not suggesting anything in particular, Mr Sapping. I'm merely pointing out what could have happened." Inspector Thomas was feeling drained. "You were in love with Blanche. You wanted to marry her but knew there was no way she would leave her husband. There was only one way to get what you wanted."

Aubrey smiled at Blanche and went to stand next to her, holding onto his glass. She looked up into his face.

"To be honest, Inspector, I'm getting a bit fed up with this interrogation now," said Aubrey, his smile slipping. "Even with Walter out of the way, how could I guarantee that Blanche would agree to be my wife?"

"Inspector," said Blanche. "Aubrey was with me this afternoon. We sat, and we walked around the terrace and were even seen by your good self. Aubrey had no chance to leave my side and go to assault your son. I give you my word on that." She spoke with authority.

"With the greatest respect Mrs Sinnet, your word is of no consequence in a murder investigation. So what is stopping the two of you being in on this together?" came back Inspector Thomas. "You could have hatched the plan and carried it out between you."

Rose gasped.

"But Aubrey has already pointed out to you that it is a little too obvious. If we were hatching a plan, as you say, it would have had a little more decorum to it. We wouldn't have left any stone unturned, would we?" Blanche looked at Aubrey who weakly nodded in agreement.

His hand shook a little as he held his glass to his lips, the only outward sign he was agitated.

Blanche let out a little cry. "Oh please, whoever did this, please come forward. I shan't blame you, as I know my husband was a selfish, cheat of a man, but please don't let Aubrey or me take the rap. We are innocent."

Chapter 22

James opened one eye to make sure he was alone in the bedroom. All clear. His snoring had fooled both Gladys and his father. Perhaps he should also consider becoming an actor when a little older. He sat up and pulled back the bedclothes, swinging his legs over the side of the bed and padded to the door in his socks. He tried the door and found to his delight that it hadn't been locked yet.

Slipping on his shoes, which someone had kindly cleaned already, he eased the door open and stepped out into the dark corridor, making his way stealthily to the top of the stairs. He could hear the murmur of conversation coming from below and noticed a light blazing under the door of the drawing room. He needed to get down the stairs and out of the side door before anyone saw him, or else his plan would amount to nothing.

As quietly as possible, he padded softly down the stairs, hoping that none of the stairs would squeak and give the game away.

James had a first-class plan on how to catch the murderer. Unfortunately for them, James had fallen forward after being hit on the head, and whoever it was had not had time to turn him over and hunt in his pockets for the weapon. Someone must have been coming their way and disturbed them. Anyway, whatever the reason, James had come to with a splitting headache and the gun still in his pocket. He had gingerly taken it out with his handkerchief so as not to disturb any fingerprints and had wondered where to hide it. There was no way he was going to go to the house to look for his father with it on him. He could be accosted on the way.

Poor James had been almost frightened out of his life as it was, without the added nightmare of taking the gun into the lion's den so to speak. He wrapped it up in his rather grubby handkerchief, waiting until it was dark and then dropped it into a plant pot under the drawing room window before making himself known.

Back to the present, though, how to get out of the side door quietly without being detected. He twisted the key, which he was glad to find in the lock, and inched it open little by little, hardly daring to breathe and wondering how to silence his exceptionally loud heartbeats that he felt must be booming out across the hall. He slipped out and made his way down the path by the light of the moon that was sporadically moving in and out between the clouds, swallowing back down the feeling of terror creeping up on him and waiting to pounce. It was easy to feel like a hero when tucked up in bed, but being outside in the open was a different thing altogether, especially as he was pretty sure the murderer would at some point come outside and hunt for the gun in the bushes.

Giving an involuntary shiver he looked around wildly, trying to figure out where the best place was to hide, unsure as to how much time he had left. Eventually he decided to stay as close to the house as possible. That way, he could yell out if needed and be heard. Also, if he could just get a look at the murderer as he or she crept out, he wouldn't need to get too near them but could slip back inside and find his father. Ducking down behind the bench on the terrace, James hid himself as best he could, trying to get as comfortable as was humanly possible on the hard ground. He settled down to wait for the inevitable, a thrill of excitement rising up inside him. Why oh why hadn't he put on a coat?

He glanced up at the house and almost screamed out in fear. The hairs stood up on the back of his neck for a second. He was being watched from that upstairs window. Who on earth was it? He had to get out of there fast, but his feet felt as if they were glued to the ground and his eyes were hypnotised by the figure, which was not moving at all. Once again his heart began hammering painfully inside his chest. Who was it staring like that? What did they want? Suddenly a light dawned in James' head and he laughed shakily to himself. Why, it was only that horrible suit of armour upstairs! He wondered if it had been put there in the first place to scare intruders away.

Back in the drawing room, Blanche was still imploring the murderer to own up. Tears were coursing down her face as the shock of the entire weekend began to catch up with her.

"Oh Mother, Mother, don't cry," cried Rose in a distraught voice. "Tell her it will be fine, Harry." She turned her face wildly towards a tense Harry.

"She's right Mother. Nothing can be proved against yourself or Aubrey." Harry took her by the arm and directed her to a chair, sitting down beside her. "Rose, get Mother a drink, quickly."

Rose raced across the room to the sideboard and poured Blanche a large brandy and took it over. Blanche was flapping at her face with her lavender scented handkerchief, trying not to pass out.

Inspector Thomas circled the room, hands clasped behind his back, taking in the scene before him. Someone was lying, but who was it? He felt something needling him at the back of his mind, but the atmosphere and chaos in the room was preventing it coming clearly into view. He needed some space to be alone and work it out.

Outside, a wispy white fog was crawling along the ground devouring everything in its path. Its tendrils pulled it along, climbing and creeping furtively across the terrace showing no mercy to any prospective victims. James was shrouded in it, feeling it clammily glide across the surface of his skin and tug at the roots of his hair. He shrank lower to the ground, his face peering up through the slats of the bench seat, waiting for any sound or movement to come from the house. He hoped the murderer wouldn't be suspicious to find the side door unlocked. No, surely not, he was just being paranoid.

The police constable responsible for searching the house for the gun had been drinking a cup of hot and reviving tea in the kitchen with Gladys and the cook to try and keep himself from getting too sleepy. Cook had even let him have a large slab of her delicious fruitcake, and she usually guarded the cake tin jealously or so the butler had told him. It had been a somewhat long day and it still wasn't over. He hoped his wife wouldn't mind him staying out for the night, but it was his duty to keep an eye out for anyone acting in a suspicious manner. He hadn't been able to find the weapon inside and wondered if it could still be outside. It would be good for him if he could find it. Perhaps it could even mean a promotion.

The stolid looking policeman drew himself up, went out of the kitchen door, and stood stock-still in the dark, the fog swirling noiselessly around his knees like a snake coiling itself around its quest ready to squeeze it into submission.

"Now, if I wanted to hide a weapon, where would I hide it?" He remained close to the house and then skirted the perimeter, feeling around in all the plant pots he passed. Stealth, that was what was needed. Stealth, a clear head and intelligence; he had them all in abundance. Ah yes, that murderer had better watch out, because Police Constable Turner was here. Putting his large hand into the last plant pot, he was surprised to feel more than just damp earth. There was something in there that felt suspiciously gun-like. It couldn't really be so, could it? What were the chances of him finding it like that? He must indeed be a genius policeman if so. In awe, he fished it out by the trigger between his finger and thumb, his mouth falling open from the sheer disbelief he was feeling. He blinked a few times trying to understand the implications of what he had just found, and considered rushing off to find the inspector. But first he peeped his head around the last corner of the house, towards the terrace, pretending he was nimbly stalking the criminal, and tucking the gun into the deep pocket of his uniform jacket. Through the swirling, milky-coloured fog, he thought he saw a small movement near the bench, and his blood froze, fear rising up from the very core of his being.

Chapter 23

Everyone seemed to be talking at once back in the house. A cacophony of voices filled the drawing room and rose up to the ceiling before being dispersed around the room.

"All of you, hush, I need to think." Inspector Thomas' head was whizzing around with a thousand muddled thoughts. He felt sure he had the clue he needed, but couldn't quite grasp it. His thoughts careered wildly between Hattie, Aubrey, Blanche, and Cordelia, and their stories. They were all suspicious to the extreme in his opinion.

Joseph began to get twitchy and started fiddling with his monocle again. He got out of his chair and began to pace up and down the room swinging it back and forth on its chain.

"Oh do sit down, Joseph," said Florence in a sharp voice. "All that monocle twirling is beginning to irritate me." Joseph slumped down into the nearest chair with a loud and heavy sigh.

"Let's remain calm and do as the inspector says," said Harry from his place by the fire. "No one can think straight with all this noise."

Hattie went and stood by him, staring into the fire with a distracted air about her.

George rubbed at his glasses with his handkerchief and held them up to the light to check they were clean. Cordelia gave him a small smile, looking more than a little on edge. Blanche was looking unwell, her eyes wide in her pale face.

"Please Inspector," implored Rose. "Let Mother go to bed. It's all very well for you to say we need to solve this tonight, but it's taking its toll and she needs to rest. I don't know how much more she can take."

Inspector Thomas looked over at Blanche and felt a wave of sympathy towards her, which overrode his suspicion of her guilt for a moment.

"We all need to rest," said Cordelia with feeling. "I feel certain I shan't sleep, but I just want to lie down and get out of this pressurised atmosphere. It's like a torment being in this room. Forgive me, Inspector, but you just seem to be accusing us one after the other and yet you don't really have any firm ideas."

"Yes I agree, and it's all too much for me too," said Florence. "Let us go to our rooms if we promise to remain in them once we are there."

"But what if the murderer gets up to his old tricks again," said Joseph looking worried. "I'm far too young to be bumped off."

Aubrey grinned. "Who would want to bump you off, old son?"

"Well, maybe I inadvertently know too much."

"What exactly do you know, Jo?" asked Harry trying and failing to look serious. "Have you any idea who the murderer is?"

"No I'm not privy to that information, but I might know something without realising it just yet. I could have seen something that will turn out to be a huge clue." His eyes widened.

"You could always lock your door behind you if you were scared," said George looking at him with disdain.

"That wouldn't help if Florence was the murderess," said Aubrey with a wicked glint in his eye. "He'd be locked in there with her."

Cordelia turned her head away to disguise a smile as Florence gave a start and looked across at Joseph, who was looking at her in turn with a horrified expression on his face.

"For goodness' sake, Aubrey," she said angrily. "What a ridiculous thing to say."

Inspector Thomas didn't want to let them go, but needed to be alone with his thoughts.

He looked grimly round at everyone.

"Ideally I would want you to stay here, but we just keep going round in circles and I need to have some peace and quiet so I can think. Off you go to your rooms. I will find the constable and ask him to keep guard on the landing so that I know there won't be any monkey business going on. You are all to stay in your bedrooms until further notice."

135

They all swarmed out and crossed the hall, disappearing up the broad staircase as one, voices continuing to cajole and bicker. Inspector Thomas could sense one of his headaches coming on. He felt completely drained and dragged his tired bones across the hall to the kitchen. He peeped around the door and encountered a sleepy looking Gladys talking to the cook. They were sitting at the large scrubbed table and were polishing the silver cutlery. The butler was sleeping in the high backed chair in the corner near the pantry, his mouth wide open with the cat curled up on his lap.

"Oh Sir," said Gladys noticing him suddenly. "Come in, do. We're too het up to go to bed. We thought if we kept ourselves busy it would help. Would you like a strong cup of tea?" She peered at him with concern.

"No thank you, Gladys," said the inspector, rubbing his forehead rapidly as if to erase the throbbing pain inside and looking over at Pericles who was yawning and stretching as only a cat can. "I'm just looking for Constable Turner."

"He stepped outside for some fresh air, Sir. Shall I fetch him in for you?" She made as if to get up.

"No, that's okay. I'm just going to remove one of the chairs from the dining room and take it up to the landing. When he comes in can you send him up? He can relieve me from keeping guard on the bedrooms."

"Yes Sir, I'll tell him when he comes back in. He'll catch his death of cold out there in that damp air if he stays out too long."

"I don't doubt it." Inspector Thomas walked across to the dining room and picked up one of the chairs, and then carried it upstairs, one of its legs scraping noisily across the statue half way up. Blasted thing! He set it down against the banister at the top and sat down, looking down the length of the landing towards the suit of armour at the other end. All was quiet. He rubbed his forehead again and wished he could go home and go to sleep, but he couldn't. He had to work everything out in his mind first. Something was nagging at him and he had to get to the bottom of it tonight. He opened his eyes wide, trying to stay awake.

The grandfather clock in the hall below whirred and then continued to tick rhythmically, lulling his mind into a deep hypnotic state. He got up quickly and walked down the length of the corridor and back again, shaking his arms and legs out as he went. His shoes squeaked in the silence. What was it that he couldn't quite remember? Sitting back down he took his notebook out of his pocket and began to read through the notes he had scribbled, and compared them to the notes made by Hattie in her neat handwriting.

Who was the murderer? They all could be. Every one of them had an opportunity to do it and none of them could totally account for his or her movements that night. Aubrey seemed likely, but he didn't think that it was him all the same. He was an intelligent fellow, despite his humorous behaviour, and he would be the sort of person to plan properly if he were to take a life. Blanche knew her husband had limited time left and so it was unlikely that she would get rid of him. She had been married to him for long enough and only had to play the long game of waiting it out.

Harry was a distinct possibility. He professed not to care about his inheritance, but that didn't ring quite true. Having had such a privileged life thus far it would not be easy to be left with nothing.

Rose didn't like her father, everyone could see that, but why would she shoot him? She wasn't going to inherit anything and being angry wasn't likely to send her over the edge was it? She could get married and leave Witton Park and never have to be in his presence again if that was her wish.

Now, Joseph and Florence were an interesting pair, weren't they? Already Florence had stolen her own jewels and hidden them in George's room. That was a criminal act, and she had no compunction about doing it. They had no money and Joseph had a memory of his own father being treated badly by Walter. Not only that, but Walter had promised him an investment and then changed his mind. That was very suspicious indeed. He must get Joseph's father traced, as there was a story there too.

Cordelia and George were secretive and had come to England lying about their marital status. Why make the effort and pay for the journey just to tell Walter to stop his behaviour? They had lied once, so why not twice? It would make sense that they had come with the deliberate plot to kill him.

Hattie's father had died at the hands of Walter, albeit once removed. She had every motive to bump him off. She had lied to him and also been secretive. Her sweet manner could be a cover up for a murderous heart. She already had Harry eating out of her hand, and Blanche too by the look of it. They would never suspect her.

The servants had no reason that he could find and he ticked them off his mental list. So who did he suspect the most? His thoughts veered towards Joseph and Florence and then careered back towards George and Cordelia. Of the two couples, George and Cordelia seemed most likely, but could he prove it? No. Not at present. They were pretty cool customers and not likely to crack under interrogation either.

Angry investors and local farmers fleetingly crept across his mind and then disappeared. Impossible for anyone to have got here in the storm, and if they'd arrived before it got out of hand, there would have been traces of a car having arrived and gone away again, and there was none. There weren't even any muddy bicycle tracks or footprints leading out of the driveway. He'd already checked that. The fields were waterlogged with no disturbed vegetation at the edges, according to his constable, and no obvious disturbances to the wall. It had to be pretty impossible to get over those spikes on top without injury anyway. No, he had to dismiss that theory as an impossible one.

Blanche and Aubrey came back to mind again. As soon as he had the written report from that doctor to prove that he had indeed told Walter that he probably had consumption, he would rule Blanche out. Aubrey hadn't known about that though. He still didn't think it was Aubrey, but just the same it could easily be either him or Hattie Abberton. Hattie Baker, he should say. Which one though?

What if they were all in league together? No, that seemed a bit far-fetched.

There was still that small something lodged at the back of his mind that he couldn't seem to bring to the forefront of his rambled cogitations.

His mind dashed about in an erratic pattern of disturbed thought. He grew more and more weary and longed to drift off and forget about it for now.

His eyes began to droop and he shook his head trying desperately to stay awake, but the next instant he had dropped off to sleep, his head lolling forwards onto his chest. The notebooks slid off his lap onto the floor. The clock continued to tick and then chimed the half hour.

Chapter 24

Pericles appeared from nowhere and wheedled around the inspector's chair, trying to get some attention, but none was forthcoming so he flicked his tail and went downstairs hoping to charm the cook into giving him a tasty titbit.

Another few minutes passed and then there was an almost indiscernible click and one of the bedroom door handles started to turn slowly downwards. The door opened bit by bit and a dark figure slipped out of their room. Keeping to the shadows by the wall, the figure tiptoed gingerly towards the top of the stairs, mindful of the slumbering inspector. A small noise rose up from the kitchen downstairs and the inspector shifted in his chair. The figure froze for a few seconds, hardly daring to breathe, then once again began to move forwards.

Once safely past Inspector Thomas, the figure crept down the stairs like a dark spectre and crossed the hall to the side door. Finding it unlocked, they felt a sudden suspicion in the pit of their stomach. Surely it should have been locked up by now. They took their hand off the door handle and crept away to go out of the front door instead, glad that the hinges had been recently oiled. The butler must have oiled all the hinges when he fixed the door after the storm damage. It was funny the way thoughts went off on strange tangents when the mind was stressed. They quietly made their way down the path towards the rhododendrons, keeping to the shadows at the sides, and holding an unlit flashlight close to their leg.

Meanwhile, James was feeling rather uncomfortable. He had cramp in both legs and was feeling decidedly damp. He would give it another ten minutes and would then have to get up and stretch himself. A small sound alerted him to the house, and he was instantly on edge, straining his ears for any further sound. What was that at the corner of the wall to the house? It looked like a face. A face! The hairs stood up on the back of James' neck as he blinked rapidly to try and focus on it. The fog loomed up at him annoyingly and when it cleared slightly, rolling off towards the lake, the face had disappeared.

Police Constable Turner was on all fours on the corner of the terrace, trying to remain hidden. He had definitely seen someone hiding under the bench. Were they after the gun? He crawled slowly towards the bench, keeping as low as possible under the ground fog.

James could hear the slither of Constable Turner's trousers as he made his way across the terrace in a steadfast fashion. He backed away, out from behind the bench and towards the rhododendron bushes. He would be able to hide properly in amongst the leafy branches and stay hidden until all was safe.

The grandfather clock made a noise and then the hour struck with a loud bong. Inspector Thomas woke up with a start and was momentarily disoriented finding himself sitting in a chair on a draughty corridor. He stood up, stretched, and made his way towards the suit of armour, rubbing sleep from his eyes. Where on earth was Constable Turner? When he reached the end of the corridor he looked out of the window into the dark night and gave a start. The moon had appeared from behind a cloud and illuminated the strangest thing.

Annoyingly, it disappeared back behind a convenient cloud again as if it were playing hide and seek with him, and the terrace was once again plunged into darkness. Did he really see what he thought he had seen or was his mind playing tricks on him? He rubbed his eyes and glued his face to the windowpane, peering down at the garden below. He didn't have long to wait. Once again, the moon sailed out from behind a cloud and he saw three figures outside. One was loitering by the rhododendron bushes, obviously trying to keep out of sight. Another figure was on all fours crawling backwards in a slow and purposeful way in the direction of the bushes, and the third figure was crawling slowly forward to the same location.

What on earth was going on? He had to get out there at once. Turning on his heel, he began to trot back up the corridor, noting that one of the bedroom doors was open. He hadn't noticed it before as all the doors had been in shadow. Whose room was it?

All at once something clicked into place in his mind and the nagging feeling he had felt before, was replaced with the beginnings of the realisation that he thought he knew the identity of the murderer. He began to run.

Back outside, James had reached the rhododendrons and was about to duck under the lower branches and hide inside when he heard a rustling sound. Someone was already under there! Was it the murderer searching for the gun? If that was so, who was it creeping towards him from the terrace? There must be two murderers. The murderer and his accomplice were seeking him out to bash him on the head again, and this time for good. James felt a terror inside him that he had never felt before and knew he would not be able to run away even if his life depended on it. Fear had rendered his legs helpless. He was no better than a bowl of wobbly jelly. The old joke about being alright in a trifle brought a sudden and hysterical giggle up to his mouth, and he quickly stifled it with his hand.

Suddenly, as if a light bulb had been switched on in his head, he remembered something the teacher had said at school about being chased by a bull. He had said that running away was no good as the bull would probably be able to run faster, and running would make it want to chase you even more. No, the thing to do was to make yourself seem bigger than the bull, even if you were not. You had to draw yourself up to your full height, wave your arms in the air, and bellow as loudly as was humanly possible. He took a deep breath and struggled to his feet.

Constable Turner was feeling decidedly brave now that he had the gun in his pocket. He knew he would never use it and didn't even know how. It probably wasn't loaded, but it gave him an assurance that would help him to see this adventure through to the bitter end. He allowed himself a small dream of being awarded a medal for bravery and smiled to himself.

The murderer had backed away towards the bushes, but that was fine. He would be cornered there. If only he had gone to fetch the inspector as soon as he had found the gun. There was safety in numbers and two were better than one when it came to catching a murderer. Still, it couldn't be helped, and he now had to make the best of it.

There he was over there, a tall looking chap, or so it seemed in the dark. Constable Turner could just about make out the outline of someone. That someone was practising making himself appear bigger, by stretching his arms up as high as he could and wiggling his fingers about.

Estimating there was around five feet between them, Constable Turner decided to jump on the fellow and pin him to the ground with his full body weight and then yell for help. What he would do after that he wasn't quite sure, but first things first.

He bent his knees and, swinging his arms backwards and forwards, leapt with all of his strength towards James who, in that instant, had begun to bellow like a banshee. He neatly sidestepped the constable in mid-flight and continued to use his voice to his advantage, surprising himself at the versatility of his vocal chords. His wail rang out over and over again, freezing Constable Turner's blood. He had crashed to the ground and was cowering by the bushes.

One by one the household was jolted awake by the noise, and those that had windows overlooking the terrace rushed to look out of the curtains trying to see through the dark and the fog. The others ran to their doors, pulling on dressing gowns or coats, and made their way downstairs as quickly as possible.

Inspector Thomas, meanwhile, had raced downstairs and rummaged in the hall cupboard where he felt sure he would find a flashlight. His own one was at home hanging up behind the kitchen door and he wished he had had the foresight to bring it with him. It seemed to take ages, and he felt as if he was moving in slow motion, flailing about in sinking sand. Finding one at last, between vast piles of gloves, hats and galoshes, he switched it on, wrenched open the side door and leapt out onto the terrace. He was greeted with the sound of an unearthly wailing and just about managed to stop himself running back to the house. What kind of wild animal was that?

He pulled himself together sharply and shone the flashlight towards where he thought he had heard the sound and, between the moving white swirls of fog, he saw James standing on his tiptoes with arms stretched up to the sky. His mouth was open, and he was making the most awful bovine sound with his mouth. Cringing at his feet was Constable Turner, blinking up at the glare of the light that the inspector had pointing in his eyes.

"What on earth is going on here?" he roared at them, striding across the terrace. He was with them in a few steps and grasped the constable by his collar, yanking him up to his feet. "James! Stop that dreadful noise. NOW!" James, the adrenalin still pumping around his body, subsided at once, but kept joggling about from foot to foot.

By then Harry, Aubrey, and George had joined them, having hastily slipped on their shoes. They skidded about on the muddy path, trying to stay upright and not slip over. Joseph and the others were peering out of the side door, huddled together in cold and fright.

"Is everything alright?" panted Harry, catching his breath. "What was that terrible noise?"

"I thought an animal was being strangled," cried Joseph from the doorway.

"Right you two, get inside the house," sighed Inspector Thomas wearily. "You have some explaining to do." He rounded everyone up like a sheepdog circling a herd of sheep. "Come on, all of you, quick sharp!"

They all turned round and made their way back inside, kicking muddy shoes off by the door.

Inspector Thomas glanced back outside in the direction they had come from with a serious and grim expression on his face, before shutting the side door carefully behind him. His hand hesitated on the key but did not turn it in the lock. Inside they found Gladys, the cook and the butler standing in the kitchen doorway looking almost frightened out of their wits.

"What was that unearthly wailing?" whispered Gladys in horror. "Has something dreadful happened to the cat?"

"Don't worry yourselves; it was just young James here. Please bring us all some tea in the drawing room," said Harry giving them an encouraging smile and they disappeared back into the kitchen frowning, and bristling at being dismissed in such a way. Didn't they have a right to know what was going on?

Everyone trouped across the hall to the drawing room and Harry turned the light switch on and shut the door, once they were all inside. James and Constable Turner were firmly ensconced into comfortable chairs and everyone gathered around them, chattering.

"I'd like to know what has been happening here. First of all, you were meant to have relieved me from keeping a watch on the rooms upstairs, Constable. As for you, James, I can't even begin to imagine what you were doing outside. Right, Constable, you speak first," said Inspector Thomas pointing at him with one hand and silencing the others with his other hand reminding Joseph of a traffic policeman directing cars.

"Well Sir," gulped Constable Turner, swallowing hard. "I had ventured outside to get some air and started to wonder where the gun could be hidden. I was certain it wasn't inside the house because I had searched high and low already."

He began to warm to his story and puffed his chest out like a turkey. "I put my hand into all of the pots outside just because I happened to be there. I didn't expect to find anything if truth be told, but then I came across this!" In triumph he produced the gun from his pocket and everyone gasped.

James looked slightly uncomfortable and fidgeted in his chair, an action that wasn't missed by his father.

Inspector Thomas took the proffered gun in his handkerchief and put it in his pocket, making sure the safety catch was on. "Thank God for that," he muttered under his breath in relief. "What happened next?" he said aloud.

"I peered around the corner," continued Constable Thomas in earnest. "There was a movement by the bench and I thought it was the murderer trying to get the gun back. I presumed he had hidden when he saw me come outside and so I dropped down onto my knees and began the long crawl towards him under the fog."

"That was exceedingly brave of you," muttered Joseph, shivering a little at the thought. Florence agreed and began to chatter away nervously about a time when she had been brave, but the others shushed her at once.

The constable continued with his story, basking in the attention. "I could see him through the clear patches of fog, and he was beating a retreat away from me towards the bushes. My immediate plan was to pounce but suddenly this loud howling started up and I was fair frightened, I was."

Inspector Thomas sighed, not for the first time that night. "Thank you, Constable, for your succinct explanation of the night's events. When you have time you can write that all out in a report for me. Now, I'd like to hear from you, James, please. Start talking and don't leave anything out this time."

"I hid the gun in the pot, Father. When I was knocked on the head, the gun wasn't taken as I had led you to believe. It was still in my pocket and I knew the attacker would think it was still in the bushes because I didn't produce it. I decided to trap them as they would have to go and retrieve it at some point, so I put it in the plant pot that the constable found it in." He took a deep breath and continued. "I slipped outside and hid on the terrace behind the bench and decided to wait to catch a glimpse of the murderer."

"Why on earth didn't you tell me? Something awful could have happened to you again. Anyway, how did you know they would go out there tonight?" finished his father, deciding not to scold him, as he would have liked to in case it put him off telling his story. He would save that until he had heard the entire tale.

"Well, it would have been their last chance, you see? The gardeners were going to trim that part of the garden the next day and the gun would have been found for sure, so I knew they would come out to try and get it back." Inspector Thomas nodded. Everyone else was listening with bated breath, hardly daring to breathe.

"I didn't tell you as I knew you would try to stop me. Anyway, there I was, ducked down behind the bench when all of a sudden I saw a face peering at me from the corner of the house. Then I heard the person crawling their way towards me. I didn't know it was a policeman. I backed away to the rhododendrons, but then I heard someone else behind me. Someone was already in the bushes."

Blanche shivered and clasped the nearest hand to her, which happened to belong to Cordelia. They held on tightly to one another.

"Who was it?" squealed Florence.

"I don't know. I half forgot about them as the constable here was chasing me and getting ready to pounce. As I said, I didn't know it was the police, and I made myself as big as possible and yelled like billy-o. Then, I'm glad to say, you all appeared."

"So where is the person who was in the bushes now?" asked Cordelia. "Are they still out there in the bushes trying to find the weapon?"

"They must be. You're right; they're out there trying to find the gun!"

"Then let's get back out there quickly," began Aubrey moving towards the door, but Harry interrupted him.

"Don't be daft, that must have just been Pericles sniffing about for mice. He's always hunting for something or other in those bushes. By the way, where's Rose? Don't tell me she's slept through all of this."

Everyone looked around the room as if expecting to see her. There was a short silence and then Joseph coughed. One by one they began to look at each other, a creeping suspicion beginning to dawn on them.

Chapter 25

"No," cried out Blanche suddenly. Her voice was hoarse with emotion and she glared round at everyone. "I know what you're all thinking. Don't you dare think that about my daughter! Not my little Rose, she wouldn't. She'll be fast asleep in her bed still. I'll show you." She made as if to go to the door but Aubrey put his hand on her arm and stopped her.

Everyone looked down at the floor in embarrassment, not wanting to meet each other's eyes.

At that moment, the door creaked open and everyone wheeled round in unison, but it was only Gladys bringing in a tray of hot steaming tea and some china cups and saucers. She plonked them down moodily and went back out, slamming the door behind her.

Cordelia made herself busy, splashing milk, tea, and sugar lumps into cups and stirring them with gusto before handing them out to the now silent room.

Blanche was wide-eyed, hanging onto Aubrey's arm and looking white and drained.

"Inspector," she croaked, looking at Inspector Thomas. "Can you please enlighten us as to what you think has happened here?"

"If you would allow me, I'd like to wait a few more minutes." The inspector went over to stand behind the door. He didn't mean to be unfeeling but was feeling stressed, exhausted, and unsure.

They didn't have to wait too long. The creak of the side door was heard and footsteps padded slowly across the hallway. They stopped outside the drawing room and there was a silence. Everyone stood with bated breath, and then the door handle began to turn. Florence silenced the scream that was rising up inside her by holding her handkerchief over her mouth.

The door opened and Rose appeared on the threshold, her dark hair tumbling about her shoulders. She stepped inside, her coat and shoes wet and muddy. Pericles ran in behind her, weaving in and out of her legs, making light of the tense atmosphere. Inspector Thomas shut the door behind her and stood leaning against it.

"So," Rose held her head high and ignored the inspector behind her. "What are you all doing in here then? I thought I heard a noise outside and went to investigate."

"Rose, don't!" wailed her mother, stretching her arms out towards her daughter. Rose ignored her and wandered over towards the tea tray. She poured herself a cup and stood there sipping at it.

Harry went over to her. "Why don't you tell us what you've been up to, Sis?" he said gently. Rose looked up at him and smiled. "Dear Harry. You've always been so good to me, haven't you? Always stuck up for me and always seen the best in me." She finished her drink and put the cup back down on the tray.

"Of course I've always stuck up for you, you're my sister, and a wonderful one at that. I need to know where you have been, though, and what you've been doing. You're ever so muddy." Harry's voice was still gentle but had a ring of authority to it.

"Well, I've been here of course, for days and days now. None of us could have left if we'd wanted to." She began to fiddle with the tea tray, the cups rattling in their saucers.

Harry put his hand over hers to stop her fidgeting. "Rose. Please. Tell us," he implored.

"I don't think I can, it's just too awful. Oh Harry, Mother, I'm so very sorry." All the fight seemed to go out of her.

"What have you done, Rose?" Blanche's voice was quiet.

"I think you already know that, Mother."

"No! It wasn't you. It wasn't. It was the man that was threatening your father on the telephone that morning." Blanche looked imploringly at the inspector. "Tell him, Rose. Tell him."

Rose hung her head and said nothing.

"Rose, please!"

"We had that call traced, Mrs Sinnet," said the inspector carefully. "I found out this morning. I'm afraid the man was one of the American investors but has not left his country and therefore cannot be a suspect."

"Then he must have got someone here to do it for him." Blanche was bordering on hysteria.

"It's okay Mother, it won't help. Do you want me to make a full confession, Inspector?" asked Rose, her head still held high. "I'm sure you want this over and done with now, so you can get back to your comfortable little village home and have all those other policemen patting you on the back and telling you how marvellous you are."

Inspector Thomas said nothing, standing still and waiting for Rose to continue.

"Very well, I did it. I killed him, but I didn't mean to do it."

The room was so silent you could have heard a pin drop. Even Pericles seemed to sense that something was up and curled up quietly on the window seat.

"Miss Sinnet, you have confessed in front of everyone here to killing your father and therefore I'm now arresting you for the murder of Walter Sinnet. Anything you say will be taken down and may be used in evidence against you."

There was a collective gasp as Inspector Thomas walked over to her and put his hand on her shoulder. Constable Turner took his handcuffs out of his inside pocket and passed them to the inspector with a questioning look. He shook his head and put them in his inside pocket.

Rose shrugged her shoulders. "It's a fair cop," she joked weakly. "I'm sorry, Mother. It wasn't my intention to make you unhappy. I'm sorry, Harry. I guess you all want to hear about it? Can I sit down and tell you before you take me away?" she implored. Inspector Thomas nodded, and she went to sit down on one of the chairs. Constable Turner walked over and stood behind her, hands behind his back, looking important.

Rose gave a little cough and shrugged to herself. "I could deny it," she said thoughtfully. "But I have nothing left to give. It's true... I shot him. He pushed me too far and I couldn't stand a minute more. What gave me away, by the way? It can't have been the fact that I was outside just now?" she asked the inspector as her mother knelt down beside her with tears pouring down her face.

"It was that combined with the blisters on your ankles," he said. "You saw James poking about near the rhododendrons and left the drawing room in a hurry, saying you were getting something from your room. In your haste you grabbed the nearest shoes you could find. They happened to be Miss Abberton's shoes. She had kicked them off in the hall after her quick turn outside looking at the bonfire, and the butler was going to give them a clean but hadn't got round to it yet. They were too small for you, but you slipped them on, and they rubbed away at your heels. You dashed out and when you returned, the shoes were caked in mud. You left them where you had found them. I had a thorough look at your shoes and there was nothing on the backs of them to suggest they were uncomfortable. However, Miss Abberton's shoes had the smallest trace of blood on the backs where they had rubbed away at your skin. I'm pretty certain the blood will be a perfect match for yours."

Hattie sat down looking stunned but said nothing.

"The shoes! I didn't mean to implicate you Hattie I promise," said Rose. "It's true, they were just the nearest shoes to hand, but they gave me terrible blisters."

"You hit me!" protested James in a dramatic way. "You could have killed me."

"Yes, I hit you, but not hard enough to kill you," said Rose looking at him. "I'm really sorry James, but I had to remove the gun from the bushes. It had my fingerprints on it."

"Tell us from the beginning, Sis," said Harry crouching down beside her chair next to his mother.

"Well," began Rose looking from her mother to Harry and back again. "I began to get really angry with Father at dinner the first night everyone arrived. He was goading you, Harry, going on about changing his will. He wanted to make mischief and I believe it was his intention to cut you out. I didn't for one minute think I would inherit anything from him anyway, but you had the right to. You needed to."

"But darling, that wasn't an issue to me," protested Harry but Rose put her hand up to quieten him down.

"Harry, you simply had to inherit something. You are the most honest man I have ever known and you couldn't stand the idea of being in a company with a miserable and dishonest con man like Father. That's why you kept resisting. Not because you are lazy as he kept insisting was the truth. You are well read and want to write a novel. How could you do that with no money behind you? Mr Marlin was going to come very soon to sort out the paperwork with Father, and I had little time to talk to him about it. Anyway, I got angrier and angrier and went back to confront him when everyone had returned to the house from the folly. Believe me, though, murder wasn't on my mind and never had been. He just laughed at me when I asked if he was really going to disinherit you and said some perfectly dreadful things about both of us. Then I said some dreadful things back and he got really mad. He told me how he had never loved us from the day we were born and we were just a drain on his resources and would be better off dead."

The blood seemed to drain out of Rose's already pale face and her grip on the arms of the chair tightened.

"Do you want a break before you continue?" asked Harry in concern.

"No, I need to get this off my chest now. He went to the gun cabinet and took out the gun and even wiped the glass clean behind himself. I really thought he was going to shoot me for a second; he threatened to get rid of all of us, including Mother and I was terribly scared for a while. He said he'd had enough of ungrateful hangers on, and that Aubrey was welcome to Mother. By that time he was drinking heavily and kept refilling his glass and waving the gun in my direction."

Blanche gave a little sob.

Florence grabbed Joseph's hand and hung onto it tightly.

"I knew Mother was better off with Aubrey and that all of us would be better off without him, and I told him so. By then we had moved up out of the folly and were arguing up the passageway to the boathouse. We stood in the boathouse, with him shouting and shouting, and then he put the gun to his head. I screamed out and he laughed again. The next thing to happen was that he thrust the gun into my hands and turned his back on me, facing the water.

He put his hands up behind his head and told me to shoot. It was a nightmare. He said that if I really did think we would be better off without him and his blessed money, I might as well pull the trigger and take my chances. He was sneering at me and didn't think I would actually shoot. I was shaking like a leaf. He kept yelling at me to shoot him, and he was laughing the whole time. Then he had a terrible coughing fit. I made as if to go to him, but the next thing I knew, there was a bang and a splash as he fell into the lake. I couldn't even really believe that I had done it, and ran back to the house as fast as I could in a dreadful panic, throwing the gun into the bushes as I passed.

"I didn't even know if he was dead, but if not I would be in for some big trouble. It was an accident!" She drew a breath and then continued. "I joined Mother, Aubrey, Harry, and Hattie for dinner and acted as if everything were normal. I have no idea how I managed it. You must think I am cold-hearted and cruel but I'm not. The depths of shock and denial overwhelmed me. In the evening the storm was quite full on and it frightened me. I kept imagining Father coming in, covered in pondweed, and pointing at me. I rushed in to see Mother in the night as I guessed she'd be alone, but half expected to find Father there too. Of course he wasn't there, and it was suddenly all too horribly real. I nearly told her there and then, but I felt trapped in the horror of it and went back to my room where I tossed and turned for ages before eventually falling asleep and dreaming over and over again that Father was coming to get me from the bottom of the lake covered with mud and with fish in his pockets."

"It must have been dreadful seeing him on the glass dome like that the next day?" said Harry in concern, the horror of the situation hitting home.

"It was the worst nightmare possible," said Rose. "He was dead, and I had killed him. Me! I rescue mice and birds from the clutches of the cat. I couldn't be a killer! I had to try to face the fact that I had taken a human life. Father was not a nice person, and had no compassion for anyone, but he didn't deserve to die like that. When he went into the water, the wind and the current of the lake must have carried him over to the statue and he got lodged there. That image will haunt me for the rest of my life."

"Oh Rose, Rose, my daughter, why did you do it?" cried Blanche in anguish. "If I'd only known just how unhappy you were I would have done something to help."

"What could you have done, Mother? It's not your fault. None of this is anyone's fault but my own. He made me do it, but even then it was still my choice. I could have walked away."

Rose suddenly looked terribly small sitting in the chair that seemed to envelop her.

"If I'd known I would have told you he was a sick man and that he was dying. I suspect he knew his time was coming to an end and actually wanted you to shoot him to stop his suffering. He never did anything that wasn't calculated. He was a mean, selfish man, and I shall never forgive myself," finished Blanche with a sob.

Inspector Thomas sighed sadly and went to speak, but Rose interrupted him. "It's fine, Inspector. I'm ready to go. I am willing to face the punishment due to me."

She put her wrists together to be handcuffed and smiled bravely at her mother as the cuffs clicked together.

"No jury in the land will see you hang, Rose. They will understand once they know your father was sick and was pushing you like that. We will do everything we can to help," Aubrey said.

"It's no good but thank you, Aubrey. I have to accept that my fate is now in the hands of the gods. Let's hope one of Harry's Greek ones will come to my rescue. Which is the god of help, Harry?" Rose's laugh turned into a half-choked sob. "Goodbye Mother. Goodbye Aubrey. Please take care of the family for me. Goodbye Harry. Remember that I love you. Hattie you must promise to look after him."

She was led away from Witton Park with Harry calling out behind her. "Rose, we will get together the best of the best to defend you. I'll phone old Marlin first thing in the morning. We can afford it now. You won't hang for this, he was dying, and it was his fault, his alone..." His voice trailed off, and the words, mingling with the fog, were carried off into the night, along with his sister.

Chapter 26

The next morning everyone slept in for longer than usual as they were all exhausted from the night's exploits. Harry wandered along to his mother's room and found her sitting on the bed in tears.

"Oh Harry, I'm so miserable," she said, dabbing at her eyes with her handkerchief. "I feel so completely helpless."

"I know, me too. Poor Rose must be having a dreadful time down at the police station.

"I'm finding it hard to believe she could shoot anyone; it's so out of character. Let's go and find the inspector to see what we can do to help her."

He took his mother's arm, and they wandered slowly out of the door, Blanche leaning heavily on Harry as if she had aged twenty years. They made their way downstairs and, hearing voices in the drawing room walked on past it and went straight into the morning room. Neither of them wanted to make small talk with anyone.

A few minutes later, Aubrey joined them, having had a hasty breakfast on his own in the dining room. He was carrying a cup and saucer and handed it to Blanche.

"A cup of hot sweet tea for you my darling," he said. "It will do you the world of good."

"I can't understand it, even now," said Blanche taking the tea gratefully and balancing it on the arm of the chair. "It just doesn't ring true somehow."

"That's because you're her mother, always seeing the best in your children, and I commend you for it. However, you have to face up to the truth now. She admitted to it and poor Rose will be punished for shooting Walter, you know. We have to be brave."

Harry looked at Aubrey in annoyance. "I don't believe she will be punished, Aubrey. When the jury hear what happened I think she will be acquitted. He tormented the poor girl. He tormented everyone. Witnesses will flock forward to testify against him."

"Maybe, Harry. Let's hope so, but there's no need to get Blanche's hopes up as we simply don't know how things will pan out."

Inspector Thomas walked into the room just then.

"Inspector," said Blanche getting up and speaking in a business-like manner. "How is my daughter doing this morning? When can I go to see her?"

"Good morning Mrs Sinnet. Your daughter is having her statement taken down at the station at the moment and Mr Marlin is on his way there. You will be notified once you can go and see her."

"What do we do in the meantime?"

"There isn't really anything you can do, I'm afraid. By the way, I sent Mrs Brewer's jewellery down to the village to be valued first thing and just had the telephone call back to let me know the outcome. They were fakes as we heard from Mr Brown."

"Oh dear, poor Florence."

"Indeed. Right, well I need to tie up a few loose ends now. It's all formalities though."

"That's okay, Inspector. Feel free to use the house as if it were your own and take your time. You may stay as long as you need to," said Aubrey graciously.

Blanche looked at him with an irritated expression on her face. "I think it's for me to say that, Aubrey," she said.

"Yes, of course, I'm sorry," he said looking abashed. "Actually, I think we should maybe talk about our future. I'm aware it is a bit soon after Walter's demise, but the sooner we get married the better. You don't need to worry about anything from now on; I'll take care of you, Blanche. You know I've always wanted to."

"Married?" Blanche gasped. "Whatever are you thinking of, Aubrey? I haven't even buried my husband. My daughter is in danger of hanging for murder, and you want to get engaged? No, I'm sorry. That is not anywhere near the way I'm thinking right now." She bustled crossly out of the door, taking her teacup with her.

Harry looked at the floor, embarrassed. Aubrey went over to the window and looked out, his hands in his pockets.

"That told me didn't it, Harry?" he said, not taking his eyes off the view. "I felt sure she would agree at once."

"It is a bit soon, Aubrey," said Harry, feeling uncomfortable. "Let everything settle down first. It sounds like you've waited a long time for her, so a little longer won't harm. Mother has a lot to take in."

"I don't like to be kept waiting, to be honest." Aubrey's voice had a hard edge to it. "It doesn't suit me."

"She's in shock. Her life has changed beyond recognition and has been emptied of her husband and daughter, Aubrey."

"Yes. I see that, but nothing can be done about them now." He began to whistle quietly under his breath.

To stop himself from saying something he might later regret; Harry turned to the inspector, who was still in the room and listening intently.

"So what will happen to the gun now, Inspector?"

"We will hold onto it for the time being, Sir. It will be used as evidence in the trial."

"The trial!" Harry shuddered.

"Yes, it won't be an easy time for you I don't suppose. Your mother will need your support."

"That should be my job," said Aubrey between his teeth, swinging around to face them. "I will be all the support Blanche needs. She will rely on me." He clenched his fists to his sides.

Harry and the inspector exchanged glances and there was a silence for a few seconds.

"Anyway, regarding the gun, I don't want it back," said Harry vehemently. "Please make sure it is destroyed when it's no longer needed. I'd hate to see it displayed in that gun cabinet again. To be honest, I may well get rid of all of those guns."

"They certainly can be a temptation to those of unsound mind," said Inspector Thomas in a quiet voice.

"I've never liked the things, not even as display objects. I couldn't be more of a pacifist if I tried!" Harry began to pace the room.

"I'm pretty much in agreement with you I have to say. Without them my job would be considerably easier."

"Then that settles it for me, the guns are going. Today! As I said, please make sure the one that killed my father does not come back to Witton Park. I couldn't bear to see it again."

"It wasn't a great gun anyway," said Aubrey under his breath, turning to look out of the window again. "The trigger was way too stiff."

Inspector Thomas, who had been making his way to the door, wheeled round and looked at Aubrey. "What did you say, Mr Sapping?" he said sharply.

"I was just saying that the gun's trigger was stiff."

"Was it? Tell me how you would know about that."

Aubrey looked round warily. "Well, I was looking at the guns when we went to the folly for a drink the other night."

"No you weren't, Aubrey," said Harry with a frown on his face. "Father never let anyone handle his guns and the cabinet was always locked. When did you get to look at them?"

"Well I... well I..." spluttered Aubrey, looking faint. "Walter showed them to me I tell you. What's with the impertinent questions?"

"When?"

"When what?"

"When did he show them to you, Aubrey? If you have nothing to hide you'll tell us." Harry's face was filled with anxiety as he spoke.

"I don't really recall when exactly it was, but he did show them to me. We had quite a conversation about them if you must know. I may well be thinking of the last time I stayed here. Yes, that's what it must be; I recognised it when the constable took it out of his pocket last night. I know a bit about firearms and recognise them better than I recognise faces!" Aubrey tried to lighten the tension with humour but neither Harry nor the inspector smiled.

"Father brought that gun back from America recently," said Harry in a steely voice. "There is no way you would have seen it before or known about the stiff trigger."

Inspector Thomas watched the blood slowly drain out of Aubrey's face.

"Mr Sapping? Do you have anything you'd like to say to us?"

"No of course not. This is preposterous. I can't remember the exact moment Walter let me look at his guns, but I distinctly remember looking at that one and thinking to myself that it had a stiff trigger. What are you trying to insinuate? Rose has already admitted to the murder of her father."

"Yes, but why did she do that? It is possible she may well have been covering for someone; someone who she mistakenly thought might have committed the crime. I'm afraid that unless you can give me a proper reckoning as to when you handled that gun, I will have no option but to take you to the station for further questioning," said Inspector Thomas in a firm voice. "There are some things that need to be cleared up."

"This is ridiculous and I am most offended. Any more of this and I shall take my leave of this house and not return to it ever again." Aubrey looked from the inspector to Harry and back again, his mouth gaping open and shut like a goldfish in a bowl.

"Mr Sapping, as you cannot give me a satisfactory answer to my question I have no choice but to ask you to come along with me."

For a split second the three men stood still looking at each other and then Aubrey suddenly made a bolt for the door. He cannoned into Harry and nearly sent him flying. Inspector Thomas lunged at him and caught him by the bottom of his suit jacket and brought him crashing down to the floor. Aubrey scrambled up again, swearing profusely, but Harry jumped on him and pinned him to the floor while the inspector took Constable Turner's handcuffs out of his pocket and clapped them on to his wrists. Aubrey swore at them profusely.

"Get your filthy hands off me. I shall make sure you are fired for this. This is the most disgusting treatment I have ever had the misfortune to receive. As for you, Harry, don't think I shall want anything to do with you anymore. Both of you are going to pay for this mistreatment."

Hearing the rumpus, Florence barged in at the door and gave a little scream when she saw Harry and Inspector Thomas manhandling Aubrey in such a way.

"What's going on here? Joseph? Joseph? Where are you?"

Joseph appeared at the door, his napkin tucked into this collar and his mouth falling open in surprise when he saw the scene before him.

"What in the name of everything that's decent is going on here? Stop it! I say chaps, stop it at once," he called out in his best thespian voice.

Much later that afternoon, Inspector Thomas appeared back at the house and asked everyone to meet him in the drawing room. They all filed in and sat down, looking at him with interest.

"Well, Inspector?" Blanche sat forward in her chair in an expectant fashion.

"We have had a full confession from Aubrey Sapping. He shot and killed your husband I'm afraid, Mrs Sinnet."

"What?" Blanche looked at a loss and gazed at Harry imploringly.

"Inspector, please can you explain?" Harry picked up where Blanche had stopped.

"I can indeed Sir. Mr Sapping picked up the gun and became a murderer. He hadn't come here with the intention of killing Mr Sinnet but..."

"What about Rose?" interrupted Blanche. "Are you really saying she didn't do it?"

"That's exactly what I'm saying. She didn't do it, as you say. Rose thought that you had killed your husband, Mrs Sinnet."

"Me?" gasped Blanche in shock.

"Yes, and she was covering for you. She preferred to hang than see you punished."

"Oh my goodness, I can't quite get my head round this." Blanche covered her hot face with her hands. "Why would she think I had done it?"

Cordelia and George got up and went over to her, each putting a comforting hand over hers. She smiled weakly at them.

"Rose did go back to confront her father about the will, and they did have the argument she told us about. Mr Sinnet even waved the gun about and held it to his head. However, Rose took fright when he gave it to her and told her to shoot him, and she ran back to the house, throwing the gun in the rhododendrons as she passed. She heard a rustling noise near the bushes as she ran, but didn't stop to see what or who it was. Aubrey Sapping was there and had witnessed the whole thing. He picked the gun up from under the bushes and then went to do what he had been on his way to do, and that was to tell his nemesis he wanted him to divorce Blanche so that he could marry her. He found Walter still in the boathouse, staring at the lake.

"By all accounts, Walter taunted him and refused to do what Aubrey was asking of him. Aubrey brandished the gun and waved it threateningly at Walter, but Walter just laughed at him and that's when Aubrey saw red. He had been meaning to return the gun but ended up shooting in anger and killing Walter. He wiped the gun clean so that his prints were not on it and then threw it back into the bushes where Rose had thrown it.

"Rose heard the shot as she was going back into the house and rushed up to her room, looking out of her window to see if she could see anything. She caught a glimpse of her mother out in the garden calling Pericles and was convinced that she had shot her father. It was then that she decided not to let her mother get caught. Everything else she said was true. She saw James by the bushes and went out and knocked him over the head to stop the gun being discovered and Blanche's prints found on it. However, James fell heavily forward and she couldn't move him to get at the gun and had to leave it where it was. She hoped any prints would be wiped away by James as he handled it.

"Aubrey wasn't worried about the gun being found, as he knew his prints weren't on it. He had wiped them off. Last night, Rose went out to try and retrieve the gun and that is when she was accused and apprehended."

"Did you know that it wasn't really her that had murdered Walter?" asked Cordelia curiously.

"No. I have to admit that I really thought it had been her. This case did not include my finest hour of detection I'm afraid."

"Did Aubrey really intend to let Rose hang?" asked Blanche in a sad voice, her eyes filling up with fresh tears.

"I think he did. He didn't want her to hang of course, but he wanted you, and he wanted to live a life of luxury. That was far more important to him than anything else. His greed overshadowed any decent bones he may have had in his body."

"So what happens now?" said Harry.

"I'll tell you what is going to happen now," sang out a voice from the door. It was Rose.

She looked tired but entirely happy.

"Harry is going to marry Hattie and we are going to be one big happy family."

"Rose!" Blanche and Harry rushed to her and threw their arms around her, laughing and crying at the same time.

George and Cordelia held hands and grinned at the scene before them, and Hattie wiped away a small tear from the corner of her eye while smiling all over her pretty face.

"What a wonderful ending. I never did like that Aubrey Sapping," said Florence. "Way too over-confident." She squeezed Joseph's arm lovingly and his monocle fell out, swinging on its chain.

About Salema Nazzal

Having always had a love for English, Salema qualified to teach it as a foreign language and then went abroad to work in Lebanon. She taught adults at a language centre and eventually ended up helping at a school on the site of an orphanage where she met her husband. She wrote about the plight of the orphans and the article was published in the centre-spread of a Christian newspaper.

Salema has been obsessed with whodunits since she was a teenager and was challenged to write her own by her sister Jess. Not knowing where to start she took herself off to college to do a crime writing course with published crime authors Lesley Thomson and Elly Griffiths and hasn't looked back since.

She currently lives in West Sussex where she takes care of her husband, two children and two cats (not necessarily in that order!)

Connect with Salema Nazzal

via author's website www.salemanazzal.co.uk or

www.facebook.com/thefollyunderthelake or

PSP Featured author's page
http://www.pneumasprings.co.uk/Featuredauthors.htm#Salema Nazzal